TRAN 59372087882778
WITHDRAWN

WORN, SOILED, OBSOLETE

D1791958

The Gentlemen's Tailor

The Gentlemen's Tailor

a novel

Mariana Leky

Owl Canyon Press

© 2010 by DuMont Buchverlag, Cologne (Allemagne)
Original Title: Die Herrenausstatterin

Translation Copyright 2013 Eugene H. Hayworth

First Edition, 2013
All Rights Reserved
Library of Congress Cataloging-in-Publication Data

Leky, Mariana.
The Gentlemen's Tailor —1st ed.
p. cm.
ISBN: 978-0-9834764-9-8

2013939680

Owl Canyon Press
Boulder, Colorado

The translation of this work was supported by a grant from the Goethe-Institut which is funded by the German Ministry of Foreign Affairs

No part of this book may be reproduced in any form or by any electronic or mechanical means including information storage retrieval systems without permission in writing from the publisher, except by a reviewer, who may quote brief passages for review. Neither the authors, the publishers, nor its dealers or distributors shall be liable to the purchaser or any other person or entity with respect to any liability, loss, or damage caused or alleged to be caused directly or indirectly by this book.

For My Parents

"I suggest that you trust me."
The Masked Man in Frank Wedekind's *Spring Awakening*

See You Later

Things could have very easily just continued as they were, but then everything fell apart. As Blank said later, that was a sure sign that things couldn't have continued as they were, even if I believed they could. What you believe, as Blank also said later, is sometimes irrelevant to the question of whether or not something needs to fall apart.

In the mornings, when I woke up, Jacob had already been back for a while, or else he had never even been gone. He'd be lying beside me in my bed, under a sheet or a blanket, depending on the season. Jacob slept like a corpse and therefore he needed a long time to wake up completely. Often he overslept and would only wake up when the receptionist called and said, "You really need to come in now; the office is full of suffering patients." Then, still half-asleep, Jacob would pull on his clothes, would go off half-asleep and would buy a take-out coffee on the way. He did it without saying a word, because they knew him in the coffee shop; he would come into the office half-asleep and cross half-asleep through the full waiting room. His receptionist knew that in the mornings Jacob was grateful for every word that he did not have to say or hear, so she wouldn't say anything, would follow him into the operating room, take the crushed Styrofoam coffee cup out of his coat pocket, hand him his freshly washed lab coat and, just before the first suffering patient came in, silently point to the sleep in the corners of his eyes. It's disconcerting to be treated by someone who still has sleep in his eyes.

Jacob was a dentist. I got to know him when I was having trouble with my teeth, which is why I knew all about dentists and really had no desire to meet any new ones. I knew about the waiting rooms, filled mostly with people who look as if they only came in for a checkup. I knew the dentist's welcoming handshake: a short, firm grasp with a hand colorless and soft as wax from so much washing. I knew the dentist's impatient nod when you were still trying to tell him something before you had to open your mouth and couldn't say anything else. You've already begun to speak in the doorway to the dentist's office, in order to say everything you have to say in the short distance between the door and the dentist's chair, getting flustered in your attempt to speak as quickly as the dentist wants you to; you rapidly describe the location and the strength of the pain and you assure him that you really do floss every night and use dental sticks, interdental brushes and the water pick, because you want to be on good terms with somebody who is probably going to make sure that the visit will be painful. Unfortunately, you always forget that the dentist isn't interested in your assurances. The dentist wants you to explain even more quickly, preferably omit the assurances and finally open your mouth.

I knew the sentence that dentists always use when your mouth is finally open: "We'll have to see each other again a few more times," they say, before they begin the examination. And I knew about the dentist's subsequent silence. Apparently dentists have not been taught that some things are less painful if you are told what, why, and how long the pain will last. I knew the blank look dentists get when they're busy with their drills, which always sound like a fax machine that you've dialed by accident—only much louder.

Once, when my previous dentist was on vacation, I went to see his stand-in. The stand-in was Jacob, who I called Dr. J. Wiesberg at the time. No one sitting in his waiting room was there only for a regular checkup.

When I first saw Jacob he looked well-rested; my appointment was in the early afternoon. As he greeted me with a welcoming handshake a tear ran down his cheek.

"Are you crying?" I asked, because the unexpected emotion surprised me. Besides, it's disconcerting to be treated by a crying dentist.

"I'm not crying," he said. "My eyes are just too dry." He pulled a little bottle out of his lab coat pocket and held it out to me. *Tears Again*, the label read, and Jacob explained that he had to put the drops into his dry eyes every so often, which meant that from time to time a tear would run uncontrollably down his cheek.

I turned the bottle in my hands and didn't know what I should say, since no dentist had ever revealed anything about himself to me, and finally I said, "It has a user-friendly design." Jacob nodded and smiled at me. I gave him back the bottle and began to say all the things I wanted to say as quickly as possible before I opened my mouth. Jacob did not nod, not at all, but asked constructive questions. He looked at my teeth, muttered some letters and numbers and said: "We'll have to see each other again a few more times."

"Please raise your hand right away if you feel any pain, and we'll stop right away," he said as he began the examination, and then: "And now, just think about something pleasant."

Because the opportunity presented itself I thought about Jacob, because Jacob was pleasant, even though he was a dentist. Jacob drilled away at my tooth and repeated several times that I should raise my hand right away if I felt any pain, because then we'd stop right away. He said it earnestly and emphatically, as if we were not at a dentist's appointment, but on a particularly daring expedition that no one had ever attempted before me. Jacob explained in great detail what, why, and how long the pain might last; he wasn't a bit reticent. "You're really doing wonderfully," he said, although it wasn't particularly painful. "You're getting through this with flying colors," he said. "People who have such a high tolerance for pain are rare," and, "you're handling this with the tranquility of an Indian yogi." He said all of this earnestly and softly, and now I finally understood why Jacob's waiting room was so full. I was happy to have stumbled onto Jacob, of all people and—even when I started to feel a little pain—I didn't raise my hand, but looked instead at a big sign hanging on the ceiling above the dentist's chair. In large letters it said: *Soon it will be over.*

In fact, it was over soon and, in fact, no one had any idea that the thing with Jacob was beginning at that exact moment. It is both totally normal and totally outrageous that we never have any clue when such affairs are beginning. At first we never have any idea of the extent and the impact of it or about what, why, and how long it will be beautiful or painful, and I wish I knew what would have happened if the sign above the dentist's chair had said *This is the beginning* instead of *Soon it will be over*. If it had said, *That's Jacob. This is the beginning, and it will be a very, very long time before it's over.* And: *It will be beautiful, more beautiful than anything has ever been before, and then it will be painful, more painful than anything has ever been before, but unfortunately, by then it will be too late to stop right away.* If it had said exactly how beautiful or painful it would be, I wish I knew what would have happened if I could have read all that on the sign above the dentist's chair while I had a drill and a suction unit in my mouth and Dr. J. Wiesberg was concentrating on fixing my tooth.

Maybe nothing would have been different and I would have only been surprised that I, of all people, would end up with a dentist. Maybe I would have been happy about the part with the unprecedented beauty, and maybe, about the part with the unprecedented pain, I would have thought, "Well, we'll see about that," like a normal dentist says when you start telling him about dental sticks and brushes as soon as you enter the office.

When Jacob woke up in the morning I was already gone. I got up early and went to translate. I worked from Monday to Friday in an office full of cubicles, where I translated instruction manuals, reports, brochures and leaflets, advertising inserts, and profound sayings and every now and then a sign. There was a lot to translate, and there was a boss named Bengt. Bengt is a name that sounds like a bouncing ball, when you yell it several times in a row, and people called Bengt's name a lot. "Bengt! Bengt!" somebody would call out when he got stuck on a translation. And then Bengt would come. He had a fast, bouncing gait, and he always looked like God was dribbling him like a basketball.

We had regular work hours and I had my own desk, but there was not a photo of Jacob on it. I didn't have anything against putting one there—plenty of people in our big cubicle office had photos of their loved ones or animals on their desks, but Jacob thought that it was bad form to put your loved ones in a frame and was convinced that I thought so too.

Evelyn, the translator who worked beside me, thought my desk looked bare. On hers there were photos of various men and women in colorful frames, large and small, and past loves and current loves and aunts and nephews, and, all year long a bowl full of Christmas marzipan. Evelyn got the marzipan from her admirers. Because she had so many admirers she had started to put on weight, and she had decided to stop eating all of the marzipan herself. She brought these gifts of marzipan into the office; she put some on her desk for anyone who wanted to take it and gave the rest to her colleagues, so we could keep them for her until the effect of all the marzipan that Evelyn had already eaten had worn off and she had room for more.

But the effect of the marzipan was persistent. And so were her admirers. Somehow they managed to find Christmas marzipan all year long, even in June.

Recently, Evelyn had more than marzipan on hand. She also had pills, which she distributed to her colleagues when needed—to make you sleep or to keep you awake, for example—because one of Evelyn's admirers was a psychiatrist. The psychiatrist was crazy about Evelyn and that's why he was doing everything wrong lately. He told all of his melancholy patients about Evelyn and her beauty instead of listening to them, the ones who had come to him because they wanted to talk about how they didn't have an Evelyn and absolutely no beauty in their lives at all, and they wanted to be interrupted from time to time by a constructive question from their psychiatrist and get prescriptions for pills that would make up for the absence of beauty in their lives, but the love-sick psychiatrist would hardly let them get a word in edgewise, and he didn't pull out the prescription pad or ask any constructive questions, and the melancholy patients grew even more melancholy as they listened to all the stories about what beautiful thing Evelyn had done or said again today, and they grew ever more suicidal.

The psychiatrist had a locked medicine cabinet full of pills, but for Evelyn he opened everything.

Evelyn translated from Spanish, I translated from English, and we seldom called Bengt. During breaks we sometimes smoked in the bathroom and talked about the easy or complicated translations we were currently working on, and about Evelyn's easy or complicated romances. After we finished smoking we'd spray a mixture of mouthwash and waterproofing spray into the stall, three puffs, a mixture that had worked well for us in the past.

Jacob and I didn't live together, but Jacob had a spare key to my apartment, and when I came home in the evening he was usually waiting for me. His hands were white and soft from too much washing; he still smelled like disinfectant and I still smelled like waterproofing spray, both odors fading.

Jacob often went for walks at night. "See you later," he would say, and when it was later he would come back. Until it was later I sat at my desk writing, translating, whatever needed to be translated by tomorrow. Sometimes Jacob would call me while he was on his walks, from some late-night main street or side road, a pub, a park or a forest if he had gone for a drive out of the city. He would tell me who he had met: a friend, a colleague, a suffering patient, a fox. He would ask me how things were going with my translation, and I would tell him whether it was coming along all right or not; usually it was.

Sometimes Jacob would take me along with him on a night-time walk; once we went for a walk along a forest path. It was pitch black and I bumped into Jacob, because I had misjudged the distance between us. Jacob stumbled and hit his head on a branch. "Oh," I said, "you were a lot closer than I thought." Jacob rubbed his forehead. "I always am," he said.

Because some things are easier to ask in the dark, when the other person can only dimly see you, there in the pitch-dark forest, I asked Jacob if he could imagine living with me. For a long time I'd wanted to live with him, but I'd never had the nerve to ask him because I couldn't imagine that Jacob could imagine it. But now, in the forest, it seemed to me that you can never really be sure what you know about somebody else, what you know about his imagination, that sometimes you just assume you know someone, but it seemed to me that you at least have to ask, so that you don't find out one day, when it's already too late, that he actually wanted the same thing the whole time, so that years later, when he was an old man lying on his deathbed, Jacob wouldn't tell me how it had bothered him his whole life that we'd never lived together.

I asked Jacob if he wanted to live together. Jacob laughed, put his arm around me, and said, "God forbid." Then he stood still and cleared his throat. "But as an alternative, I'd suggest that we get married."

I often planned for absurd things. I imagined crazy things and planned for them, but the idea that Jacob would want to get married was so absurd that even I hadn't planned for it. I'd assumed that getting married was even worse in Jacob's opinion than having framed photos of your loved ones, and no forest, no place in the whole world, could have been dark enough for me to ask Jacob to marry me.

But now I wished I could see Jacob more clearly. "Of course," I said, "Yes, of course." Jacob put his arm around my shoulders. "Good," he said, "Then we will."

We walked on in silence, and then we stumbled over a tractor tire and fell headlong, sprawled out flat on the ground. We just lay there for a long time without talking, because neither of us could quite grasp the idea that we were getting married. Then, once our eyes had adjusted and we could judge the distances better, Jacob looked over at me and smiled. "Fantastic, isn't it?"

"Absolutely," I said.

We got married at a lake. Jacob had chosen the vows. "*Set me as a seal upon thine heart, as a seal upon thine arm: for love is strong as death,*" said the pastor. "*Its coals are coals of fire; it is a flame of the Lord. Many waters cannot quench love, neither can the floods drown it,*" he said, and he repeated it around midnight when he had fallen into the lake, drunk and happy.

Jacob's mother and my father gave speeches; they stood in front of our table with pieces of paper trembling in their hands and talked about what Jacob and I had been like as children and when we were growing up, then everyone applauded and gave toasts.

When Jacob was a child, his mother said, she had had to take him to the emergency room all the time for bandages or casts or stitches and once, when he was just a year old, the doctors had had to save his eye at the last second, because he'd looked into a bottle of Drano that wasn't closed properly. One time he'd ridden his tricycle right into a mass of barbed wire so tangled up that they had to cut him out, another time he was running along the cobblestone pavement with a noisemaker in his mouth, and when he fell it got stuck in his throat. He'd fallen out of tree houses and bunk beds, and when he was only eight months old he'd crawled into the stormy Mediterranean, and he'd only been saved from drowning at the last second.

My father talked about how I'd been a cautious child, how I'd almost never fallen down, because I spent most of my time sitting at the kitchen table and painting. I painted pictures with bright, happy colors. My father always said, "Why don't you paint a monster, or a crow, or at least something dark?" but I kept right on painting in my ice cream colors, unperturbed.

Jacob had forged his parents' signatures on letters when he got into trouble at school; he'd dumped trashcans on teachers' heads as they were climbing the stairs. Jacob had some real behavior issues, his mother said with a smile. As for me, my father said, I'd tended the school vegetable garden and tended to my friendships, and any time I got a B, my teachers asked if I was very disappointed.

When he was in college, Jacob had only done a half-baked job of studying for his exams, if he studied at all, but somehow he'd always passed them. His mother said it was probably because people always liked to hear Jacob talk, even when he wasn't talking about what he was supposed to talk about. That was true. When I was in college, I was always thoroughly prepared for my exams. "She was always very ambitious," my father said. That wasn't true—I didn't study because I was ambitious—I studied because I was anxious, and when you're anxious you confuse the important things with the totally absurd things, so I was thoroughly prepared for even the most absurd questions, and the night before an exam I'd always drink so much calming herbal tea that I had to go to the bathroom all night long.

During my vacations, which were never far from home, I would always take walks that were supposed to have wonderful views at the end, but then I'd take a wrong turn and find myself in some quiet residential compound that didn't have much to offer except the certainty that I'd taken a wrong turn somewhere, which is why, my father said, when people asked me about my vacation, I'd always give monosyllabic answers. Jacob, his mother said, would always run into danger on vacation. He'd claimed it was an accident when he wandered off the path in a Siberian forest full of bears; he'd claimed it was an accident when he got locked in an African national park full of crocodiles overnight, and both the bears, which Jacob played dead for, and the crocodiles, which Jacob ran away from, had just had babies, and so they were even more dangerous than usual.

My father said that the first thing I'd told him about Jacob was that he wanted to live in a tent. "Imagine, a tent!" I'd said it in outrage, and added that I was the kind of person who'd prefer to live in a big single-family house with shutters on the windows.

At the end of her speech, Jacob's mother said that Jacob and I were an adventure for each other in the best of senses. Jacob whispered, "Watch out, here comes a metaphor," and Jacob's mother said that for Jacob, I was the house with shutters that he'd never dreamed of and for me, Jacob was the tent that I'd never dreamed of.

Jacob's tiny grandmother, who looked like glass and was hard to understand because she and her vocal cords were one hundred two and a half years old, pulled herself up from her seat to say that we were the most harmonious couple she'd ever seen. Then she started crying, and everyone applauded, and Jacob went over to her, picked her up like a fragile vase, and set her on his lap. She sat there until all of the speeches, the eating, the presentations, and the applause were over, and it was finally time to dance.

There was a lot of dancing at the wedding, a lot of drunken chaos, a lot of crying. Jacob's grandmother wouldn't stop crying about the fact that we were such a harmonious couple; Jacob's second cousins cried because they had been arguing and didn't know how to make up; Evelyn cried because she'd realized she was in love with Bengt, with Bengt of all people, but Bengt wasn't in love with her anymore; Jacob's sister cried when they played her favorite song for the second time; my mother cried because she was so happy she was still around to experience all of this; Jacob's niece cried because she was in love with Jacob; my aunt cried because she wasn't in love with my uncle anymore; the pastor cried because he found his speech so moving; Jacob's mother cried because Jacob's father had not lived to see all of this; my niece cried because the son of Jacob's best friend from school had stepped on the hem of her new dress and ripped it. There was always somebody standing at the edge of the dance floor and crying, but not for long, because someone would always go right over to them and comfort them and pull them back onto the dance floor, and then they'd start dancing again.

There was also a lot of disorderly kissing. Evelyn kissed an orthodontist and hoped that Bengt would see it, but Bengt didn't see it, because Bengt was off among the reeds kissing my godmother, who told him with red cheeks that that was out of line and she was much too old for him. But he did it anyway. The drenched pastor tried to kiss my mother, but that was truly out of line. My niece kissed the man who had stepped on her dress, and after she kissed the orthodontist, Evelyn kissed Jacob's uncle by marriage, who was now divorced again.

By dawn some people had left, others were sleeping next to the tables, or on them, or under them, still others were talking quietly or slow-dancing without music. Jacob, Evelyn and I walked out to the dock and lay down, my head on Jacob's stomach, Evelyn's head on my stomach. The paper lanterns above us rustled quietly against each other in the night wind, the frogs croaked in the reeds, a rowboat tied with a rope rocked back and forth on the lake. Evelyn sat up, took the last swig from a bottle of vodka that she'd been carrying around for a long time now, and looked at the boat with her lower lip sticking out. Evelyn was very drunk. "Every time one person meets another person," she said, lifting her index finger in the air, "it's like one empty boat meeting another empty boat." Evelyn had been in a relationship with a Buddhist some time ago.

Jacob laughed, Evelyn leaned backward, let her head drop onto my stomach, mumbled something else about Bengt and boats and empty and drunk as a skunk, and fell asleep.

Jacob's French friend from college had brought along his seven-year old son, who came running over to us sleepy-eyed and wished me and Jacob a happy new year for the umpteenth time, not knowing how to wish us anything else in German. "Thanks," we said. The sleepy-eyed kid sat down next to us and skipped stones across the water. Jacob ran his fingertips back and forth along my collarbone; everything was peaceful now, the only things I heard were the croaking of the frogs, the little waves, the skipping of the stones, the sounds in Jacob's stomach. I lifted Evelyn's head, turned on my side, and laid her head on my hip as my eyes slowly closed. Just before I fell asleep, I heard Jacob whisper in my ear, "We did a good job," and I saw someone standing on the other side of the lake smoking, someone I could only dimly see. I'm sure it was just a lone wedding guest or a fisherman, I'm sure it wasn't Blank, it couldn't have been, because he never smoked, but still I sometimes imagine that it was Blank who was standing there smoking on the other side of the lake, looking over at Jacob and me. I imagine that because I wish that Blank could say, "I know. I know; I was there, I saw."

As a wedding gift, Jacob's favorite aunt had given us a five-foot-tall porcelain pink flamingo. Its curved neck looked like one half of a heart, and it stood on one leg, with the other leg curled up and its right wing outstretched. His aunt had meant the flamingo ironically, but that didn't make it any smaller. Jacob wanted to throw it away immediately; he wanted to leave it on the side of a country road as we were driving back from our wedding. Jacob was sitting in the passenger seat with the flamingo between his legs. There wasn't any space left on the back seat; it was full of other bulky gifts. The words *Just Married* were written on the rear window behind the piles of gifts, Jacob's mother had sprayed them there in gold spray paint and no one knew if they would wash off.

I didn't think we should ditch the flamingo, because I think we should always hold on to gifts, especially gifts from those you love. "Even when their gifts make us suffer?" Jacob asked.

The right wing of the flamingo was resting on Jacob's knee; the head was on his shoulder. Jacob was trying to reach around the flamingo to put bandages on his feet, which had been crammed into new shoes for the whole wedding.

"'Suffer' seems a little bit melodramatic in this case, doesn't it?" I asked. "And besides, you do love your aunt."

"I love my aunt, but I don't love her gifts. And if you love someone, can't you tell them the truth?"

"Of course," I said. "But not if the truth is completely unnecessary and would only hurt your aunt's feelings."

"But this flamingo is completely unnecessary, and it's hurting me," Jacob said, and he pushed away the flamingo's head, which kept trying to nuzzle against his neck.

"Maybe it will break soon. It looks pretty expensive," I said, because the more expensive porcelain is, the more likely it is to break.

"We'll put it in the cellar," Jacob said.

"What if your aunt comes to visit?"

"Then we'll bring it upstairs."

"What if it's a surprise visit?"

Jacob's aunt came to visit frequently, and she'd been known to drop in on me as well as Jacob unexpectedly.

Jacob had finished bandaging his foot, and he leaned over and kissed me. "You take it," he said.

We put the flamingo in my living room. Jacob tried to make it look like an accident. Several times a week he'd bump into the flamingo, stumble on it or lean up against it as if inadvertently, but even when the flamingo fell over, it didn't break.

"Let's put it in the garden," Jacob suggested. "That will wear it down." We took the flamingo down to the yard. Jacob put it behind a fir tree, where nobody would see it.

"But it's too sheltered behind the fir tree," I said, and moved it to the middle of the garden. "We have to expose it to the weather."

We went back upstairs and looked down at it from the window. Now the flamingo was fully visible, standing there on one leg in the middle of a flowerbed. "I hope it doesn't take long," Jacob said. But it did. The flamingo lasted for more than two years.

That fall, when hundreds of chestnuts rained down from the tree but somehow missed the flamingo, almost all of the employees at Bengt's translation agency came down with the flu; only Evelyn and I remained. Bengt took some of Evelyn's pills for insomnia and he hopped nervously around our desks and kept asking if we could work any faster. After I spent four sleepless nights in a row translating, Jacob decided to help me translate in secret after he got off work. "That's fraud," I said. "It's an emergency," he said. "And after all, everyone speaks English." He spent several nights translating brochures and ad slogans, slipped me the translations in the morning, and when I showed them to Bengt, he said he was a little shocked that I, of all people, was suddenly making so many careless mistakes, but he was pleased to see that I'd worked up the nerve to make my translations freer and more creative.

That winter, while a neighbor kid was trying to build a snow flamingo next to our porcelain one, but kept running into trouble by the time he got to the neck or the dangling leg, Jacob's sister died of an especially virulent type of cancer. Before she died, she spent a week in intensive care. Jacob sat on a stool next to her bed day and night, holding her hand and crying, as if all of the fluid that his eyes had been missing before was coming out now, all at once. I stood behind Jacob to catch him when he dozed off from exhaustion. Whenever he nodded off, I'd hold him with one arm around his upper body and the other hand bracing his head, the same way I held him later at the funeral, when he went off on the pallbearers in a fit of tears.

In the rainy spring, when a puddle had formed on the flamingo's back where a blackbird bathed now and then, Jacob flew off to America for three months. We wrote to each other every day. I counted the days. When I went to the weekly market, I would think, "Just six more weekly markets until Jacob gets back." When I was shopping at the supermarket, checking expiration dates, I'd think, "By the time this cheese goes bad, Jacob will be back," and at some point there were just two more weekly markets to go, and at some point it was only long enough for butter to go bad, and then yogurt, and then fresh milk, and by the time the sun had bleached the flamingo so much that it wasn't even pink in some spots, just a sort of faded rose, Jacob was back. He'd brought gifts and stories with him, he'd had a lot of experiences, he'd given completely impromptu speeches about dental prostheses, he'd gotten into danger a number of times in American national parks, and suddenly I was shocked to realize how little I'd experienced while he was gone; I'd been so busy waiting for him to come back that I hadn't experienced any more than was absolutely necessary.

The next winter, when a thin blanket of snow coated the flamingo's outstretched wing, there was a plague of rats. The rats came into the cellar from the street—you could hear them squeaking at night. I would only open the apartment door far enough to squeeze in or out, then I'd close it again as quickly as I could. "They won't come into the apartment," Jacob said, "no rat can make it up four flights of stairs."

"Are you sure?" I asked.

"No, but it's absurd."

"That's not an argument," I said.

One night when I opened the toaster oven to put in a pizza, a rat was sitting right there, looking at me. We were eye-to-eye. I closed the door of the toaster oven, took my bag, and left the apartment. "I'm not going back in there," I told Jacob. "I know," he said.

I never went back inside that apartment. Jacob spent the weekend packing my boxes with some friends, and at night I'd massage his shoulders. One night, while I was massaging Jacob's shoulders, it occurred to me that in principle this would be a good time for us to move in together after all. Jacob took my hand from his shoulder and kissed it. "I'm not moving in with you, dear," he said, "just in case that's what you were thinking." "Jacob, you're all knotty and tense."

As we were loading my boxes into the moving van to take them to my new apartment, Jacob said, "The flamingo. This is a good opportunity." We were tired, and we thought we'd held on to the gift long enough, and since now even Jacob thought that people who love each other should keep the truth to themselves when it's an unnecessary truth, especially when it's not only unnecessary, but also years too late, we decided to tell Jacob's aunt that the flamingo had gotten smashed in the course of the move, so thoroughly smashed that it couldn't be glued back together. We left the flamingo in the garden; we didn't even turn around to look back at it.

Two days later, my old landlord called. Jacob and I were lying in bed in my new apartment, between boxes that I hadn't unpacked yet, and it was unpleasant to talk to the landlord on the phone while I was naked.

"You left your bird in the garden," the landlord said.

"The bird. Right," I said. "We're going to pick it up."

"Please do. As soon as possible," the landlord said.

Jacob wrapped his arms around me from behind. "You can just throw it away," he said into the telephone beside my ear.

"I'm not authorized to do that," said the landlord. "And besides, it's too big; it would have to wait for the next bulky item pickup."

"Then chop it up," Jacob said, "so it'll fit in the regular trash."

"I'm not authorized to do that," said the super. "Why don't you chop it up yourself?"

"We're not authorized to do that either," Jacob said.

A few days later, Jacob's aunt dropped in to see me unannounced. She thought the flamingo looked ironic the new garden, too.

The next summer, as I was wrapping a vine around the flamingo because Jacob had heard that vines have a destructive effect, Jacob said, "Hey, it's our anniversary. Let's go on a trip." We'd gotten various gift certificates for our wedding for canoe trips and balloon trips and wellness weekends, and they were all lying in a box unused. One of the wellness weekends hadn't expired yet. So we went to a hotel where the rooms didn't have any corners and there were whale songs playing in the swimming pool. Jacob sang along. In the evening he pulled me onto the hotel bed, put the complimentary chocolate into my mouth, and took off my clothes. "We could actually conceive a child right now," he said.

"I think we'd have to move in together if we had a child," I said. "Then I guess it wouldn't work," Jacob said, and smiled. His naked back was reflected in the black screen of a TV, which was the only thing in the room that had corners, aside from the complimentary chocolate.

"I've been thinking about it. I could move in with you. You have a garden, so I could stay in my tent now and then."

Jacob moved in with me, and now and then he stayed in his tent. A lot of his patients lived in my neighborhood, and they raised their eyebrows whenever they saw him crawling out of his tent in the morning next to a life-sized flamingo ""I think the patients find you strange," I said, and Jacob said, "I think they find the flamingo even stranger."

In the fall, when the dried-up vine had almost completely fallen off of the flamingo, when it was only dangling from the flamingo's neck, so that it looked like the bird was getting ready to hang itself, there was one morning when Jacob didn't come out of his tent. I knocked on the flap. Jacob didn't react. I unzipped it and crawled in. Jacob was sitting on his air mattress with his cell phone in his hand, he was pale, and he looked at me as if he could see through me.

I was startled, and I knelt down in front of him. "What is it?" I asked.

Jacob put his cell phone in his pocket. His voice was hoarse. "I'd like to stay with you, if possible," he said.

"Of course it's possible, Jacob," I said. "Why wouldn't it be possible?"

Jacob took me in his arms and held me tight, the cell phone in his pocket beeped to announce a new message, Jacob held me so tight that it made me dizzy, and weeks later, when everyone had forgotten about it and Jacob had disappeared entirely, the flamingo actually fell apart. It didn't fall apart gradually like I'd expected, but all at once. Blank was there; he saw it from the balcony, suddenly the neck broke, suddenly the beak and one of the wings fell off, just like that; nobody had even touched it. "The ornamental flamingo in your yard fell apart," Blank yelled over to me. "Was that actually yours?"

I ran out to the balcony, looked down at the garden, and started to laugh. I laughed longer than I'd ever laughed before, I laughed so loud that it almost scared Blank. I wiped the tears off my cheeks. "Finally," I said.

Jacob's disappearance began gradually, and at first I just couldn't see him clearly. Jacob was getting blurry. "I can't see clearly anymore, Jacob," I said.

"You're just too tired," he said.

But my vision didn't clear up, and I started to miscalculate a lot of things. I miscalculated the distance to Jacob, and the distance to doors and furniture. I misjudged the width of steps and the height of doorsills, and I was always stumbling over something or bumping into someone. "Excuse me," I was always saying, sometimes even to doors, furniture, and doorsills, and when I finally knocked out a tooth stumbling against something, Jacob said, "Maybe you really should get yourself checked out."

He didn't say much else anymore. Most of the time he didn't speak—he hadn't been speaking much for several weeks now—because there was something particular that it took all his strength not to say. I didn't speak either. We kept on not speaking about that unspoken thing, and it took hold of us the way an abscessed tooth can when it's left untreated, the whole immune system is preoccupied with that one inflammation and doesn't have any time or strength left for the rest of the body.

I didn't know what Jacob wasn't telling me, and at first I kept asking questions. I asked him if he was very unhappy, if his vocal cords were inflamed, if there was someone else, but since he had to keep quiet Jacob just nodded in response to the first question and shook his head to the second and the third.

When Jacob went out at night, he didn't say "See you later" anymore, he just said "See you." And when I did see him it was always the next morning, and I'd never been able to sleep, because I was always trying to figure out what Jacob wasn't telling me. I thought of the most obvious and the most absurd possibilities, but since I always misjudged the distance to Jacob, I never figured out what it was that he was keeping quiet about, even though there were signs, like the fact that he always headed for the shower as soon as he got home, or the fact that he kept getting letters in colorful envelopes with no return address. Still, I didn't think of it, maybe because it seemed too absurd, or too obvious, or just because it was unthinkable.

Sometimes I paced back and forth in Evelyn's apartment, bumping against tables and chairs and even against Evelyn, and wondering aloud what had happened to Jacob, and how Jacob and I and our love could still be saved. Evelyn said, "He's found someone else. All signs point to that."

I ran down the list of all the signs that pointed away from it, and Evelyn didn't say anything, she just looked at me as if I were an inventor who couldn't give up on an ostensibly revolutionary invention, even though everybody knew that it didn't work.

Jacob treated the tooth that I'd broken when I stumbled; he didn't say that I was unusually brave, or that I was like an Indian yogi, he didn't explain what would hurt or for how long. I tried with all my might not to look at the ceiling, because I knew the sign there would tell me that it would be over soon.

When I was sitting in the optometrist's chair, the optometrist told me that I needed an operation. After the operation, Jacob sat next to my bed in the hospital. Now I wasn't just seeing badly, I wasn't seeing anything at all, because I had a cool, soft bandage over my eyes that felt like eyeglasses made of snow.

Someone came in and said that he was the doctor and that everything would heal wonderfully, and I'd be able to go home in a few days, but it would be two or three weeks before my vision cleared up completely. The doctor patted me on the shoulder and left.

Jacob and I didn't say anything, we'd brought our whole silence of the past few weeks into the hospital room with us; it could only fit because we made ourselves very small. At some point I heard Jacob stand up. "I can't do it anymore," he said.

I knew that whatever it was that Jacob had been diligently keeping quiet about for the past few weeks, whatever it was that we had been diligently not thinking about was about to come out. It wouldn't take two or three more weeks, it wouldn't even take a couple of minutes. In my head I heard a sound like a fax machine that you get when you've dialed a wrong number, but much quieter. Jacob said, yes, there was someone else, her name was Alina, and he didn't know what she meant to him, or how much.

"I can't see you, Jacob," I said.

Maybe it didn't even mean anything, Jacob was saying, maybe Alina was just a symptom, a symptom of the fact that something wasn't right between us anymore, but maybe she was more than that.

"Jacob, stop it. I can't see you," I said.

Jacob said that he just hadn't been able to tell me, but now he couldn't take it anymore, and I tried to pull the bandage off my eyes, but it was stuck too tight.

Jacob said he'd move into a hotel for now, and then he said he'd better go, but then he didn't go.

"Jacob?" I asked, since I hadn't heard him leave. He didn't say anything else. Everything was quiet, but I could tell that he was still in the room. "Jacob?" I asked again. He didn't answer. I felt sick.

"Is someone there?"

Jacob didn't answer, but I heard him leave.

Two days later, Evelyn picked me up from the hospital and took me home.

Whenever Evelyn was working on a particularly tricky translation, I would reassure her by saying that before the yogurt she'd just bought had expired, she would have forgotten all about the translation. There was a bottle of aspirin in her car. Evelyn held it close to my eyes and said, "By the time this aspirin expires, the pain will be gone."

The expiration date on the aspirin was a year off. I looked at Evelyn like a blindsided inventor. This love was real, this pain was just as real, and it couldn't be squeezed into a single year.

I opened the door to the apartment. It wasn't easy; I fumbled with the lock as if I were drunk. Jacob wasn't there. I looked for him in every room. I stumbled against chairs and doorframes.

I sat down on the bed that until recently had been Jacob's and mine. The silence was so loud that I had to cover my ears. Suddenly it occurred to me that Alina might have been in that bed sometime while I was away, and I ran out of the bedroom as if there were a plague of rats in it. I stumbled against a cabinet. I was glad that I'd stumbled against the cabinet, because the sound broke the silence, and I sat down on the sofa and wondered if Jacob really was in a hotel, and if he was, whether he was alone in the hotel, or if he had booked a double room and Alina was there with him right now, if that symptom of the fact that something wasn't right between us anymore was there with Jacob in that double room right now, making it clear to him that she wasn't just a symptom, that she was actually the only effective medicine.

I thought about the pastor at our wedding, how he'd said that love should be set like a seal upon the heart, and I wondered if maybe that was the problem, that it's better not to seal love or to stick it fast at all, or maybe it should only be sealed with spit, maybe that would hold better. I thought how the pastor had said that even water and floods can't quench love or drown it, because love is the flame of the Lord. I wondered if Alina was an especially powerful flood, a flood more powerful than even the Lord himself had ever experienced, maybe the Lord had carelessly thought that a flood like that was too absurd to even worry about. I wondered if Alina was a symptom of the fact that we'd been fooling ourselves and the flame of the Lord was easier to quench than we'd thought, just as easy to quench as a normal, unreliable campfire, a candle, a tea light.

On the way home from the hospital, Evelyn had urged me to get mad at Jacob, she said it was only appropriate, and besides, it could be purifying, and in any case it was healthier than brooding, brooding was a poison, especially when you were inconsolable. But I didn't get angry. Instead I spent the whole night thinking about all that I could have done better, about all that I could still salvage, about Alina, even though I didn't know anything about her, about Jacob, even though suddenly I didn't know anything about him either. Suddenly, it seemed to me, I didn't know the slightest thing about Jacob anymore, even though everything was full of Jacob, the whole apartment was full of Jacob, and by the next morning I felt like I'd dug a deep pit inside myself, a toxic waste dump, and filled it full of poison.

Every day I ran through sentences in my mind that I still wanted to say to Jacob. Sentences that might yet save everything. I called Evelyn. "I absolutely have to call him," I said. "Call him as often as you want," she said, "but wait at least two years."

Every day I tried to work until I was exhausted, but since everything looked like a blur to me and I couldn't concentrate, I couldn't work very well. I hoped that Bengt would find my translations daring and creative, just like Jacob's, but Bengt thought they were miserable, so he said, "Why don't you take a vacation."

I wanted to tell Bengt that there was no way I could take a vacation, that I couldn't do without my job, that I needed money and I needed something to do, that I urgently needed some way to kill the time, to kill more time than it takes even aspirin to expire, and that he should give me something else to do, that I could answer phones or clean the office or dust everyone's photos of their loved ones.

"A vacation sounds great," I said.

Some evenings Evelyn would drop by. To distract ourselves, we'd play a game called "City, Country, River," and once we had named everything from A to Z except X, we'd come up with a new category. Evelyn, who still wanted me to get angry, proposed the category "Murder Weapons." "Never," I said.

Evelyn brought me a book that her psychiatrist had written. It was full of positive catch-phrases that the psychiatrist had come up with, you were supposed to stand in front of the mirror and repeat them aloud. At night I stood in front of the mirror with the book. The catch-phrases were all about making positive choices—choosing joy, choosing fulfillment, choosing love. I delivered all my lines without much conviction, all except for the line about choosing love, because I really had chosen love, it's just that I'd chosen a love that I couldn't have anymore. I looked at my face in the mirror. I didn't look like someone who'd chosen fulfillment; I looked like someone who'd gotten trapped in an elevator that was stuck between floors.

I looked at the water stains next to the mirror and decided to scrub the bathroom. It's never a good idea to scrub your bathroom when your vision is blurry. But still, it's sometimes a good idea to do something that doesn't require anything but scraping and scrubbing. So I scraped and scrubbed all night, and the whole time I kept trying to come up with a country that started with an X.

At two-thirty in the morning I went out to the newsstand. I was wearing sunglasses; I always wore sunglasses when I went outside because of the bruising from the operation.

When I came back into my building, I saw a man sitting on the landing. I could only see him dimly, the light in the entryway was always flickering because of faulty wiring, and my sunglasses made everything dark anyway. When he saw me, he stood up.

"Good evening," he said. "Don't be scared."

I went up the stairs. The man was an older gentleman in a black suit.

"Can I help you?" I asked.

"No, thank you," he said.

"What are you doing here?"

"Just taking a little rest."

When an older gentleman takes a little rest on the landing, it sometimes means that he's having a heart attack or some other terrible problem with his fragile heart, but this man didn't look like he was having any problems with his heart, he didn't look short of breath, or fragile, he just looked tired, certainly very tired.

"Are you sure you don't need help?" I asked just to be safe.

He smiled. "I'm okay." He looked at the bare light bulb flickering on the ceiling and then he tried to see my eyes through my sunglasses. "Is it too bright for you?"

"No," I said, grabbing the railing for support, because I'd suddenly realized that I was very tired, too.

"Would you happen to know a country that starts with X?" I asked.

"No," he said firmly, as if he'd been thinking about it for a long time. "There isn't one. Sorry."

"Well then," I said, "see you later," and I walked past him and up the stairs.

"Excuse me," he called when I was halfway up the stairs.

I turned around. He stood on the landing, tall and thin, his hands folded across his stomach. "I'm sorry," he said. "I'm very sorry."

I pushed my sunglasses up closer to my eyes. "Thanks," I said, and as so often happens, outrageously often, in fact, I had no idea that right then, right at that moment, something new was beginning.

I finished scrubbing the bathroom and fell asleep in the bathroom with a paint roller on my stomach. I slept for more than four hours for the first time and woke up in the morning, because the doorbell rang. Evelyn was at the door, an open bag of marzipan in her hand. "Good morning," I said, and admitted that there was no country that started with an X; there was not one far and wide in the entire world.

"There is certainly *one*," Evelyn said, chewing. "But it's probably extremely small. And extremely remote."

She pointed to my white speckled face. "You got a tan," she said.

And then my phone rang. I was sure it was Jacob. I had done everything possible so that, if and when Jacob finally called, I would not miss it; I had set the phone to the maximum volume, activated the vibrating alarm and all the light signals, and finally, when I had scrubbed the bathroom and also the category for a country that began with the letter X, finally Jacob called. I pulled the phone out of my pants pocket. *Jacob's cell phone calling*, it said. "It's Jacob calling," I said to Evelyn. I waved the phone around in front of her face; the phone rang and vibrated and lit up and I was beside itself with joy. "I choose love," I said to Evelyn. "And I also choose happiness and abundance." Evelyn said: "Don't answer just yet," and I said, "You have a few screws loose."

I pressed the green button and beamed at Evelyn. "Hello," I said as calmly and cheerfully as possible, and as if I didn't know who was calling. "It's Alina Eckert," said Alina.

I pressed the red button and threw the phone on the floor in the hallway. It immediately began ringing again, blinking and vibrating, and because a vibrating phone can move by itself, the phone began to move slowly towards me.

"It's Alina," I said to Evelyn.

Evelyn picked up the phone and answered it. "Hi, this is Evelyn." She said something unintelligible, because she had two pieces of marzipan in her mouth, "and you must be the symptom."

Then Alina spoke and Evelyn listened. Then Evelyn stopped chewing and spit out the marzipan into her free hand. Then she hung up without saying a word. Then she said: "You have to go to the hospital right away."

The driver who was responsible for the accident was sitting on a bench outside the ICU. When he saw me, he stood up and took off his cap, a flat cap. We stood facing each other; the driver who was responsible for the accident was a head shorter than me. His face was expressionless, waxen, his mouth half open as if he were asleep. He did not say a word and stroked my shoulders with both hands over and over again, mechanically, as if he wanted to smooth out something that had been sewn crookedly.

I looked over the head of the driver who was responsible for the accident into the face of the doctor, who asked if I was the wife. She said that it had happened this morning and she was solemn and put a hand on my shoulder. Because the hand of the driver who was responsible for the accident was also stroking my shoulder, she laid her hand on his and said something about liability that the driver who was responsible for the accident missed, and about severe internal injuries. I said: "Jacob is always a little drowsy in the morning."

The doctor glanced past me, because someone was coming down the hallway behind us. I turned around. There was a woman, carrying Jacob travel bag; she sat down on the furthest bench. In her hands a coffee trembled; she glanced up at me; she cried and wiped her hand over her nose and she was incredibly beautiful.

Evelyn took the hands of the driver who was responsible for the accident from my shoulders. He dropped his arms, as if someone had turned him off.

The doctor put her arm around my waist and pushed me along the corridor. I turned around. "You are incredibly beautiful," I said over my shoulder to Alina and I was surprised that I addressed her formally, and the doctor led me into Jacob's room.

Jacob's face was purple and swollen. His body was covered with signs of his internal injuries, the back of his head bandaged, and also the left side of his face. There was a tube stuck in his hand; he was surrounded by equipment which periodically emitted light signals. The doctor squeezed my hand and left the room.

I sat on the edge of the bed and stroked the back of Jacob's bandaged hand. I leaned forward and held my mouth to his ear; Jacob didn't smell like Jacob, he smelled like blood-soaked gauze; there was dried blood stuck behind his ear. A strand of hair was caught in it.

"Jacob," I whispered as quietly as I could, "Jacob." Jacob turned his head toward me. The white of his un-bandaged eye was red. He tried to keep the eye open, but it was difficult. "It's you," he whispered. He whispered it neither with surprise nor disappointment nor relief; he whispered it like a child who repeats a sentence without understanding it.

There was a knock on the door, the doctor poked her head in and asked if everything was okay.

"He's awake," I said and laughed. "He's awake. Everything is okay." The doctor came into the room, looked at Jacob and then the equipment. She laid a hand briefly on my shoulder and walked out of the room.

I ran my index finger over Jacob's collarbone, back and forth, back and forth. "It's you," I whispered.

It was difficult for Jacob to speak; he took a long time to say something. Finally, the sentence was finished.

"Something funny has happened to me," he said.

Jacob tried again and again to keep his red eye open but it was no longer possible; again and again the lid fell down like the wings of a tiny and very tired bird, and then all the light signals were blinking faster, then noises came from all the equipment that were much louder than any fax machine and much more resolute.

"See you later," Jacob said, and then he died.

The doctor, Evelyn and I walked down the hospital corridor. The light was blinding bright; I pushed the sunglasses closer to my eyes. Evelyn and I went over to Alina and the driver who was responsible for the accident, who were still sitting on the bench in the hallway. The doctor paused. Evelyn and I went on to the hall door, where we stood and waited for the doctor; I looked at Evelyn and myself, reflected in the glass of the door, and reflected behind us, the doctor, the driver who was responsible for the accident and Alina who, when the doctor had finished speaking, placed the coffee cup on the floor, sat up very straight and then no longer moved. The driver who was responsible for the accident covered his face; I heard him howl; he winced and turned toward me, the howl of the driver responsible for the accident sounded like the cry of a donkey. The doctor patted his shoulder, then walked over to us and took us to the main exit.

The older gentleman in the black suit, who had been sitting in the stairwell at night, stood just outside the clinic door. He stood in front of a waist-high funnel-shaped ashtray for patients who still smoked.

I stopped. "What are you doing here?" I asked. His face was contorted. He tried to find my eyes behind my sunglasses; he stretched a hand out, as if he wanted to caress my cheek, pulled it back and ran his fingers through his hair instead.

The doctor gave me a long look and reached into her coat pocket. She pulled out a bottle that looked at first glance like *Tears Again*, and handed it to me. "It's okay to take this," she said, "it's completely homeopathic."

I said goodbye to the doctor, I said goodbye to the gentleman in the suit, and, as we took a seat in the car, Evelyn opened her purse and pulled out a small piece of paper which contained two pills from the locked medicine cabinet of the love-struck psychiatrist.

"You don't need homeopathic medicine. What you need is something reliable," she said. "This here will make you light and tired in no time at all."

I wanted to go home. Evelyn drove me home. "Should I come up with you?" she asked.

I shook my head. Evelyn gave me an inquisitive look. "That's not necessary," I said. "Really." And I wished Evelyn would stop giving me that inquisitive look. I had always been good at protesting, but now every protestation was exhausting. "Are you sure? Shouldn't I stay?"

"Yes. Absolutely. I mean, absolutely not."

I got out and went to the front door. Evelyn rolled down the window. "Call any time," she said, and: "Don't you die, too."

I put Evelyn's pills into a cup and sat down at the kitchen table.

The book by Evelyn's psychiatrist stated that if you believed you were going crazy, you should count someone's hair. Because there was only my head at the moment, I stood in front of the bathroom mirror and began to count my hair, but the attempt to count your own hair leads to madness and tension, so I stopped and sat down at the kitchen table again. I thought about all the time I had to kill now. I contemplated expiration dates that might be comparable, but none were comparable, not even the one on the tin can being sealed somewhere at this very moment, not even the one being issued on a passport somewhere at this very moment. Finally I remembered sugar, the expiration date of a filled bag of sugar somewhere at this very moment. Sugar fits, I thought, and because it fit, it was unthinkable. I stood up, in any case I could not continue to sit, and at that moment the phone rang. I ran, as if I didn't know who was not calling and who could never call again.

"I just wanted to hear your voice," Evelyn said.

"Thanks."

"And I also wanted to ask you something. It's ... it's about something very inappropriate. That's why I didn't have the courage earlier."

"Just tell me," I said. "It can't be that bad."

"You're absolutely right," Evelyn said and exhaled audibly. "It's like this: the psychiatrist has given me something for my birthday which can't easily be returned."

"Your birthday. Yesterday was your birthday. I'm sorry. Happy birthday."

"Thanks," she said, and then: "He's given me a cruise."

I certainly knew but did not believe that people still went on cruises; I thought that the last cruise ship had sailed a hundred years ago.

"It's a nice gift," I said. "When does it sail?"

"The day after tomorrow," Evelyn said.

"Oh."

"But I've already told him that I might not be able to go with him."

I stood at the window; it was dark outside and I could see myself reflected in the glass. "Smooth sailing," I said. I really wanted to say, "Stay here," but to tell Evelyn that she shouldn't go on vacation was just as impossible as Bengt saying that I shouldn't go on vacation.

"Are you sure?"

"I'm very sure," I said. "Very, very sure." I said it gladly; it wasn't a difficult assurance, it was good; the best thing I could do now was to stand at the window, reflected in the glass, and assure someone that something was very, very sure.

"You can send me a telegraph sometime," I said. Evelyn laughed.

"Well then. Try to sleep."

"Good night," I said and hung up. I imagined the cruise ship sailing away and all the psychiatrist's patients standing at the pier, the patients who were even more unhappy lately and more suicidal than they already were, because recently the psychiatrist had only been thinking about Evelyn, because he no longer listened to them and no longer asked questions, and not because they themselves did not have an Evelyn in their lives; I saw all the patients waving large cloth handkerchiefs after the psychiatrist, who was now sailing out to sea with Evelyn and with all the patients' secrets, which they knew were only safe with him now because they had become completely irrelevant.

Blank appeared in my apartment the night before Jacob's funeral, just as I was carrying back a mountain of empty glass bottles. I thought cleaning up might help, because it made me tired and it was noisy, and I badly needed to feel tired and to tackle the silence that, since Evelyn had taken off, could no longer be outsmarted by anything other than cleaning up. Because everything still looked fuzzy to me, I caused a lot of disorder when I cleaned up. In the evening I went into the basement to clean up there too, and began to wipe off a discarded aquarium. In the process I bumped into a shelf, one of Jacob's boxes fell down, and suddenly, in the middle of the basement's silence, a faint, happy music began to play. I dug my fingers into the dust rag and turned around. The music was coming out of the fallen box, from a greeting card Jacob's sister had sent to him for his birthday—a musical greeting card. It was playing *Here's to Your Life*. I threw the dust rag into the aquarium and stumbled up to the apartment, but it just didn't help to be in an apartment full of silence with a head full of *Here's to Your Life*. I piled a mountain of empty glass bottles into a cardboard box and balanced my way down the stairs with it. I felt my way step by step; I was doing okay and didn't drop any glass bottles. The glass recycling bin was on the opposite side of the road. Beside me at the traffic light stood a man with a dog. "Need some help?" the man asked. I shook my head. The traffic light was red; there were no cars to be seen. My arms trembled beneath the heavy glass bottles. I stepped into the road. "Stop!" the man cried. I jumped back onto the sidewalk; I was doing okay and didn't drop any empty glass bottles. "I was talking to the dog," the man said. The recycling bin was full; it would not hold any more glass bottles. It never occurred to me to put the box down beside it, and I balanced it back into the apartment, sat it down in the hallway and myself beside it. "Get up," I thought, as loud as possible, because it's not a good idea to sit silently in the apartment next to the empty old bottles I had just brought back inside, which solves nothing. "Get up," I thought. "Get up immediately. Don't just keep sitting here, anyway." But I thought all of that silently. My arms were still shaking from carrying the glass bottles, my legs and my head were shaking now too, and that would have been an appropriate time to take Evelyn's emergency pills, but I didn't think of it—because in the case of internal emergencies you seldom think of anything that is appropriate and right at hand on top of that—and then I heard someone clearing his throat; without a doubt someone was in the bathroom, clearing his throat.

I stared at the sign that had hung above Jacob's dentist chair and now leaned upside down against the wall in the hallway: *Soon it will be over*. It will not all be over soon, I thought, it's over *now*.

I stood up—it was easier than I thought—and took an empty wine bottle from the cardboard box. I grabbed it by the neck. I had seen on television how you can defend yourself with a raised bottle, and I was relieved that I obviously wanted to defend myself, because the desire to defend yourself argues against a secret plan to die afterwards. The bottle in my hand was shaking. "Is anyone there?" I asked from the hallway.

"Yes," said a man's voice. "My name is Dr. Friedrich Blank. I'm in your bathroom."

"Are you a dentist?" I asked, and walked quietly down the hallway.

"No," said the man's voice. "I'm a classicist."

Blank sat on the edge of the tub. He had thrown his legs one over the other and was looking intently at his hands, which were lying in his lap with upturned palms. His hair was disheveled; it looked like an abandoned bird's nest. When he saw me, he stood up. He buttoned his suit jacket and came towards me slowly.

"Please forgive me for just barging in here like this," he said, and held out his hand.

"We've already seen each other a few times," I said.

"Yes," said Blank.

"In the stairway."

"Yes."

"And in front of the clinic."

We shook hands. I examined Blank's face, a wrinkled face with bright blue eyes behind oval glasses. Blank examined my face, the bruises around my eyes from the surgery still visible. "It looks painful," he said. "Did you get into a fight?"

Only now did I realize that I was still holding the wine bottle, raised high in my left hand, and I put it down. Blank cleared his throat again.

"I'm really sorry that I shocked you. I can explain everything to you, incidentally."

"My name is Katja Wiesberg and my husband is dead," I said, and then I burst into tears.

"Maybe we should sit down for a moment," Blank said, putting an arm around my shoulder. "May I?" he asked. I nodded, and Blank led me to the edge of the tub. We sat down side by side. Blank wiped a tear from the corner of his eye.

"You're crying," I sobbed.

Because I had suddenly and finally grown very tired, I put my head on his shoulder. "May I?" I asked. "Of course Blank said. I stopped crying and stared at Blank's lapels, his white shirt collar and his thin wrinkled neck. Then I raised my head. Blank smiled at me.

"Will you explain it to me now?" I asked. "Gladly," he said. "The whole thing will seem a little absurd to you. To be precise, I'm no longer alive. I am, if you will, extremely hard to believe."

When I woke up, I was laying on the sofa. I woke up because Blank was stroking my arm, very gently at first, and then a little more vigorously. When I opened my eyes he pulled his hand away quickly and was embarrassed, the way you get embarrassed when you have to wake someone up by hand and you only know them formally. "I knocked several times," he said.

I remembered nothing, and then I remembered everything.

"It's now half past ten," said Blank. "I'm afraid that in an hour it will be time."

I sat up. I had dreamed about Alina; that she was incredibly beautiful and I told her how beautiful she was; in my dream Alina had said: "I know," and I was ashamed.

"I don't know what I should wear," I said. I ran into bedroom, trying not to look at the bed, and went to the closet. When I opened it Jacob's scent hit me. Blank sat on the edge of the bed and cleaned his glasses. "Maybe you should eat some breakfast first?"

"Better not," I said.

"Something light, maybe? You know, if you don't eat breakfast, you'll keel over."

I rummaged through the closet, found a long dark skirt of mine and a black jacket of Jacob's that was much too large.

"Will this work?"

"Of course," said Blank.

I went into the bathroom and brushed my hair. Blank stayed in the bedroom. "Please come in," I said, because I didn't want to be alone, not even in the bathroom. Blank came in and stood behind me. We looked at ourselves in the mirror, me in the black jacket that was much too large, Blank in his perfect-fitting black suit, white shirt and black tie.

"You're dressed just right for something like this," I said. Blank smiled. "Out of necessity," he said.

I put up my hair and thought about the exceptionally bad French twist the hairdresser had given me for the wedding. Jacob had picked me up from the salon, I had looked at him miserably, and Jacob had laughed and said:

"I'm marrying you with a beehive on your head."

Then we tried to muss up the utterly immovable hairdo a little, but that hadn't been easy. Blank was standing behind me silently and suddenly I stumbled, even though I had not moved my legs. Blank put his arm around me; we went into the kitchen. He took the sugar bowl and put three cubes of sugar in my hand.

"Let them dissolve," he said.

I tossed the sugar into my mouth like a tablet; the cubes melted away very slowly.

I took one of Evelyn's two tablets out of the cup.

We examined the tablet in the palm of my hand; it was tiny. "What's in that?" Blank asked.

"I don't know. Something that makes you feel light in the shortest time possible. And tired."

Blank hesitated. You could tell that he wanted to say something, something against it, something like, "Maybe that would be even worse."

Blank let his sentence slip away unsaid and got a glass of water. "To your health," he said with a slightly crooked smile. "To the pharmaceutical industry."

"I swallowed the pill down with the water. The bell rang. "I've got to go," I said and stood up. "You're coming along too, right?"

"I'll catch up with you."

"Are you sure?"

"Definitely."

"See you later," I said.

When I opened the apartment door, my parents were standing there. My mother held flowers wrapped in paper in her hand. The bouquet was very elaborate; many colorful buds peeped out. "They were lying here in front of the door," she said. I unfolded the note stuck to the paper flowers. *You too*, it said.

This time the pastor, who had fallen into the lake at our wedding, said nothing about fiery coals and streams where you cannot drown; instead he said something about inscrutability, and afterwards he did not cry, because he wasn't drunk and he had not found his speech very moving. Blank was sitting on my right. Jacob's mother was sitting on my left and she looked like a ghost.

There was a lot of crying at Jacob's funeral, but now everyone was not crying for different reasons, but for the same reason, and Jacob's mother was not crying. Her hair had suddenly turned white. I had read in an article that when something happens that is not supposed to happen, your hair may lose its color, and in another I read that this could not happen.

I did not cry. "I can't cry," I said to Blank. "Maybe it's because of the pill. Maybe I'm too light." I should have brought Jacob's *Tears Again* with me.

"You don't have any tears left," Blank said.

Jacob's coffin was standing in front of the altar. I did not cry, because I was counting on the absurd and found that as long as the casket was still standing, as long as it was not lifted, there was still time, as long as the coffin was still there, Jacob was not going away, Jacob was still there, Jacob was still possible, and when the pallbearers approached the coffin, to lift it up, I felt sick. Everything in the pit of my stomach, all of my guts, seemed to drop.

"My guts are dropping," I said.

"That's normal," Blank said and squeezed my hand. "Don't worry."

The pallbearers approached the coffin. It was now very quiet. I had to find a way to deal with the silence. I had to do something immediately; cleaning up had helped the night after Jacob died. I freed my hand from Blank's, stood up and said: "I'm going to help carry the coffin."

Because I was standing in the front row, because wives are always in the front row at funerals, nobody could turn to me, but the silence in the church grew even more silent.

I walked forward. Not only could I easily carry way too many empty bottles up and down at one time, I could also carry heavier things. When friends moved, they always called me first because I was well known for that, and I was also able to carry the heaviest moving crates, and a coffin shared by four pallbearers could not weigh more than a carelessly packed box of books. I had also taken a pill which made me feel light, and a pill that makes you feel light may also make whatever you want to carry feel light.

The pallbearer on the right in back stepped aside; I took his place.

"The other way around," the retreating pallbearer whispered. All the pallbearers were facing the exit; I was the only one facing the altar. "Sorry," I said, and turned around. One of the pallbearers said: "On three. One. Two. Three." He said this quietly, as if we were planning to scare someone on *three*. On three we shouldered the coffin.

I was shorter than the other pallbearers and the coffin tilted to one side.

On the way through the church I looked at Blank, the way you fix your eyes on something stationary in rough seas, so you won't get seasick. Blank looked at me and wiped his brow.

It went well until we reached the middle of the nave. Then Jacob's uncle jumped up and raised the coffin up on my side.

"I'll carry it with you," he said.

After the funeral I lay on the floor in the kitchen; Blank sat beside me, leaning against the sink. I told him about how everyone had offered me their condolences at the grave—his friends, his relatives, his colleagues, his assistant, the suffering patients—everyone except Alina, who had not been there, and about how I had asked myself whether I was actually still his wife, and if not, who among the ones who offered their condolences knew that as of late I probably wasn't anymore. I told him about the wreaths and ribbons of garland; of how, although the coffin had clearly been lifted and had clearly been carried, I had continued to hope for the absurd; as long as the coffin had not been lowered there was still time; how the pit of my stomach dropped as the coffin was lowered, and how Jacob's mother had thrown up on the ribbons of garland, on my arm, on the sleeve of Jacob's jacket. Blank stroked the locks of my hair gently, as if he wanted to count them. "I know it well," he whispered. "I know; I was there. I saw it."

"Can you stay for a little while?" I asked Blank in the evening; I asked it as casually as possible.

"If I'm not disturbing you, I'd like to stay for a while."

It is impolite to ask guests what they mean by *a while*, because the question implies the hope that it will be a limited amount of time, and I did not want to imply that I was hoping the amount of time Blank would stay would be limited.

"Are there other places you have to go? I mean, do you have other appointments? You can gladly take my car, if you have a long way to go. You would just have to bring it back afterwards."

Blank smiled. "I actually do have something to take care of," he said, "but that can wait. And it's not far away."

I carried the bed sheets and Jacob's bedside lamp from the bedroom and tried at the same time not to come into contact with the bed. Blank looked tired. "Then good night," I said. "If you need something, just wake me up."

Blank sat on the couch, and then he stood up again. "Will you be able to sleep?" he asked.

"I don't know."

"I'd be happy to stay awake with you."

"I was going to sleep too soon," I said. "Good," said Blank and sat down again.

I went into the kitchen because there was something there I wanted, something I could not remember when I got there. I took a sponge and tried to rub the vomit from Jacob's mother out of my sleeve. It didn't come out; it just spread and made the sleeve dripping wet. I picked up a plastic bag, went into the bathroom, and tried not to look in the mirror, the way you try not to look at a pile of unopened overdue notices. Jacob had left the least amount of stuff in the bathroom, so I started there. I took Jacob's shower gel and put it in the bag. I put the razor in the bag. The toothbrush, the toothpaste, (which was the toothpaste dentists recommend to their family); I put the dental sticks in the bag, the water pick, the interdental brushes. The gel, the comb, the callous remover. There was nothing left. It went fast.

I carried the bag into the kitchen and stuffed it into the trash; it didn't fit. I took the swinging lid off; the bag was now perched on top of everything else that should have been taken out a long time ago.

While I was standing in front of the trashcan, it dawned on me that I had no place to sleep. There was no way I could sleep in the bed I had shared with Jacob, because Alina had probably been there, and the sofa, which was probably harmless, was where Blank was sleeping. I thought about sleeping in Jacob's tent, which was still in the garden. But Alina may have been there, too. Maybe Alina was reassured by things that could be taken down quickly and without a trace; perhaps in that sense she had understood Jacob very well.

In the cabinet was the large bouquet of flowers that had been placed in front of the door. That had been nice of Alina. That Alina had done something nice made it worse.

I sat down on the floor next to the trash, looked at the stove, which stood across from me, and tried to wring out the dripping wet sleeve of Jacob's jacket, even though you can't wring out something very well when you're wearing it.

"You can't just keep sitting here," I thought, because suddenly I was not sure whether the shadowy thing I saw through the oven door was in fact the baking dish or a large, immobile rat, that was looking at me and waiting until I opened the door and we were eye to eye. "Stand up," I thought, and the voice in my head was not particularly quiet, but my legs were too light to stand, as if they were filled with air, perhaps because of the tablet, which is supposed to make things light.

I continued to sit, looked at the stove and thought about everything that was no longer possible to conceive. The sentences that I still wanted to say to Jacob, that I had invented, about everything that could still be salvaged, were inconceivable, the past was inconceivable, the present and the future absolutely inconceivable. The last few years, together with his sizeable love, were inconceivable, Alina was inconceivable, Jacob's totally red eye, and the resolute noise of the intensive care equipment. There was no direction to think in anymore, not even Bengt was conceivable anymore, Bengt, who had sent me on vacation and who, Evelyn had said with downcast eyes, had appointed a new English translator. I should get up, confront the stove, count the hairs on my head and risk tension and madness. Perhaps a temporary tension might even be helpful, because tension is a pain without a cause; perhaps even a temporary madness would be helpful, because someone who is mad is probably preoccupied with the most absurd thoughts possible, not with the obvious ones. An obvious one, for example, was that now, without love and without Jacob's life, my life was over, that which had been and that which had been waiting in the wings, and just before I thought that, Blank came in.

You could tell that he had slept—his suit was rumpled. He looked at me with a start, ran across the kitchen, crouched in front of me and hugged me, and this time he didn't ask if it was okay.

I rested my face on his shoulder. "There's nothing left anymore," I said; I said it unintelligibly. Blank said something back, it was also unintelligible, because Blank was whispering and because his mouth was on my shoulder. "What did you say?" I asked.

Blank raised his head and looked at me, let me go and stroked his hands over my face. The pressure of his hands on my face was firm; Blank stroked my face the way you would really only stroke your own face when you applied a cream. His eyes were red.

"You mustn't let yourself waste away," he said. "At least not completely."

"Could you please see if there's a rat sitting in the oven?" I asked. Blank stood up, opened the oven door and peered inside for a long time. "There is only a casserole dish in here as far as the eyes can see," he said, closed the door and sat down beside me. I had been sitting beside the trashcan for a long time, and meanwhile the wet sleeve of the jacket was almost dry and in return the dry one wet.

"He's taken everything away with him," I said. "Even what didn't belong to him."

"Should we call a doctor?" Blank asked.

"No," I said and wanted to get Evelyn's second emergency pill or ask Blank if he could get it, but to do that one of us would have to leave, and I didn't want either of us to leave.

Blank cautiously stretched out his legs and looked at me.

"But can you really know that?" he asked.

"What?"

"That there's nothing left anymore."

I nodded. Blank massaged his temples. "Are you sure that you can know that?"

"I am very, very sure that I can know that," I said, and slowly my legs grew heavier, because an assertion, after all, was a sign of life, even the assertion that life was no longer possible was a sign of life.

"I'm one hundred percent sure," I said, and stretched out my legs too. Blank's legs were much longer than mine; his black shoes looked huge behind my feet.

Blank did not stop asking me if I could really know. "Can you swear it?" he asked. "Would you bet everything you have on it?"

"Those aren't very high stakes."

"Sorry," he said. "But will you swear? Can you swear to it?"

I swore it, I swore it on demand a few more times; I protested that I could swear to it, and then I said, "No. Of course I can't be one hundred percent sure."

"Exactly," said Blank, and sighed, as if he had just taken up something very heavy, as if somebody had rushed to help him and said, "'I'll carry it with you."

"Exactly," Blank said again and took my hand, "and so it would be good if you could decide not to waste away completely."

I was looking at Blank's shining shoes; I looked closely—there was not one single tiny mark on them. Blank was trying to scratch his left ankle with his right hand, but it didn't work; he let go of my hand and scratched himself extensively with the left. "I'll tell you something," he said. "All important decisions are made on the basis of incomplete data." He had finished scratching and reached for my hand.

"Can you really be a hundred percent sure about that?" I asked. Blank laughed. "Yes," he said. "What do you have there? A nutmeg grater?"

I opened my right hand. I had forgotten there was something in it. "That's a callous remover," I said. "Jacob's callous remover."

Blank let go of my hand and took the callous remover out of my hand; I must have been holding it very tightly because the pattern was imprinted on my palm. Blank leaned over the callous remover like a watchmaker over a very small clock movement; he ran his index finger over the rough surface and tiny traces of Jacob's callused skin trickled over his leg. Blank gently stroked the callous remover over the calloused places on his fingertips.

"There are things out there..." he said.

I stood up. My legs tingled; I was dizzy; I held on to the stove.

"Are you going to sleep now?" Blank asked.

"No. But I have to lie down again."

"Yes," Blank said. "That's a very good idea. Can I do anything for you? Should I come with you?"

I smiled at Blank and shook my head.

"Should I keep an eye on the oven?"

"No," I said. "The baking dish isn't going to do anything."

"If you need me," Blank said, "I'm here. I'll just keep sitting here. With this strange grater."

Astronauts

When the bell rang at the door one night, it had, I believe, not rung in a very long time. Since Jacob's death time did not pass in the usual way anymore, and even expiration dates could no longer be trusted. Time now had strong rhythmic disturbances; it lurched forward, tiptoed in place on the spot where it stopped, sometimes raced, and not infrequently did all of this at the same time.

When Blank and I sat silently on the sofa for five minutes, sometimes in that five minutes two whole days passed. When I was almost sure that I had made it through another week, and said to Blank: "Apparently the stores are open for Sunday shopping today," Blank said, "Today, to be precise, is Wednesday."

You could tell that time, in spite of its new unpredictability, somehow passed, in the same direction it always passed, by how the complete absence of Jacob changed.

Jacob's complete absence, which at the beginning had been something pointed, piercing, deafening, had now become a large area that surrounded me like a landscape, where I had been displaced, where I'd have to transfer my principal residence, where I lost myself, especially at night.

I was sitting in the kitchen when the doorbell rang in the night. I went to the door and looked through the peephole. There was a fireman standing outside. When I opened the front door and the fireman saw me, he raised his eyebrows. I raised mine, too. We looked at each other silently with raised eyebrows, until the fireman said, "We heard your place is on fire, dear."

He said *dear*, even though we were only just now seeing each other for the first time; he said *we*, even though he was standing there alone.

"Are you from the fire department?"

The fireman lowered his eyebrows and drew them together. "Where else would I be from? May I come in?"

I took a step sideways. The fireman walked past me and he smelled like a man's cologne being offered on sale. He now stood in the middle of the hallway, looked at the four half-closed doors, and finally back to me, as if waiting for me to point to one of the doors and say: "There's a raging fire behind it."

"There's absolutely nothing on fire as far as we know," I said, even though I was also standing there alone.

"We'll see about that," the fireman said; he said it like a dentist talking to a patient who insists that his teeth are fine. He shined a flashlight in every room. "What are you looking for?" I asked. "The fire," he said.

I had no idea that there were fires you have to search for with a flashlight, but a fireman certainly knew better about that than me. Finally he went into the kitchen, opened the kitchen window, climbed on the window sill and shined the light in the gutter.

I wondered briefly whether I should hold onto him, because the window sill was only made for primroses or basil or other light things in pots. The fireman climbed back down. "Everything's fine," he said regretfully. He shined the flashlight in my face without noticing, because in his mind he was involved in something big that did not exist. I grimaced. He lowered the flashlight, took his cell phone out of his pocket and called his colleagues. "Everything's fine," he said. "We can head out."

"Would you like some coffee?" I asked, because I couldn't sleep anyway, and the fireman didn't look as if he wanted to head out.

His face brightened. "Sure," he said. He called his colleagues again, said that if there weren't any other calls he would stay here for a while, and sat down at the kitchen table.

"It kind of stinks in here," he said. He leaned back and stared at the flamingo, which was next to the kitchen window. I had wrapped the flamingo's neck and beak with adhesive tape and glued his wings and propped it up with a stick. It worked.

"What kind of a fiasco is that?" the fireman said.

"A gift," I said.

The fireman looked around, pointing here and there with his flashlight as if it was a laser pointer, even though the ceiling light was still on, made suggestions and acted as if he had just persuaded himself, against his better judgment, to buy the apartment, including the furnishings. He talked about how easily the curtains could catch on fire, as well as the PVC table cloth, which had also been a gift from Jacob's aunt, and then about everything else that was imperfect.

"The windows are pretty dirty," he said, "the chair wobbles," and "I'd put the shelf somewhere else; it looks kind of lost over there." He leaned forward, opened the refrigerator door and shined his flashlight inside. "There's absolutely nothing in there," he said, disappointed.

"I can offer you some marzipan," I said.

"Sure," said the fireman, and leaned back again. "I can imagine, by the way, how good that chest of drawers would look painted light green."

I made coffee and realized that essentially the fireman wasn't talking about the kitchen, but about me. I probably didn't smell very good; I was also a fiasco; my ability to catch on fire was no longer what it once was, and I was pretty dirty and wobbly; I also belonged somewhere else, where I would look less lost; there was also nothing inside me and you could also imagine how good I would look in light green. A leaf from a potted palm had settled on the fireman's head and it patted him imperceptibly when it moved. I took a cup and poured the fireman coffee.

"But all in all you can still do something with it," he said.

The Gentlemen's Tailor

"Thanks," I said. "Milk and sugar?"

"Jet black." He reached into the inside pocket of his uniform jacket, pulled out a roll of peppermints and a can of deodorant spray and held them both out to me.

"Thanks," I said, stuck a peppermint in my mouth and sprayed deodorant under my arms and in the kitchen. While the fireman was drinking his second cup and finishing his speech, I suddenly grew very hot. "You're getting quite red," he said.

"That's because your stories are so exciting," I answered. That was a lie. The fireman had not talked about anything exciting, just the plot of a karate movie from the eighties. Whenever he came to a climactic scene from the film, he remembered that he had forgotten to mention something which you needed to know in order to understand the climax, and then after each climatic scene he explained its meaning, and it's not easy to get thrilled about the retelling of climactic scenes from karate movies, even if you have all the information you need to understand them. In reality, I was turning red because I had remembered that the cup the fireman was drinking his coffee from was the cup that contained Evelyn's second emergency pill.

Now the tablet was inside the fireman's body. I wondered what a tablet that took effect in me against internal emergencies and was supposed to make me feel light and tired, would do in the body a fireman, and whether it could have horrible side effects, because it really belonged in a locked cupboard. I wondered whether I should call a doctor or a pharmacist, but apart from its effect I didn't know anything about the tablet, not even its name. I thought about calling Evelyn on her cruise ship, so she could ask the psychiatrist. I said, "Would you excuse me for a minute?" to the fireman, who was now already less committed to explaining the climatic scenes in karate films, and called Evelyn and wondered whether information from a lovelorn psychiatrist could be at all reliable, and Evelyn did not answer the telephone, probably because you can only send a telegraph to someone on a cruise ship. I went back to the kitchen table and wondered if a tablet for internal emergencies, inside a fireman who is supposed to be fighting external emergencies all day long, would cause him to make mistakes and because of the inner feeling of lightness fall from a ladder or a window sill; I wondered whether the fireman would immediately form an addiction to pills, to a devastating internal and external dependence on crime to support his habit; I wondered if he was allergic to the ingredients; if it was necessary to pump out the fireman's stomach immediately; and when just as I was beginning to wonder whether the fireman was going to die in my kitchen at any moment he asked, "Your coffee—is it decaffeinated?"

"No, it's full strength," I said.

"Why are you looking at me like that?"

"Sorry," I said. The fireman put his arms on the table, rested his chin on the palms of his hands, shifted a piece of marzipan from one cheek to the other, and smiled at me. "You know what," he said, "I've never been so relaxed."

"I'm glad," I said and decided to closely monitor the fireman's health. He rested his head in one palm so the entire right side of his face was pushed up, and now he no longer talked about karate movies, but about how coffee was used in breeding pigs. His grandfather, he said, had a farm with lots of pigs, but among them there was only one hog, which had to father all the offspring. "And sometimes the hog was simply too exhausted, and could sometimes simply do no more," the fireman said with a voice full of compassion, as if there had often been similar demands made on him, and somewhat indignantly, as if I had said that the hog shouldn't make such a fuss. When the hog could no longer continue, the grandfather slipped him one cup of jet black coffee. "Then he's lubricated again," the fireman said.

"I'm glad to hear that," I said.

He rubbed his eyes. "It wouldn't work so well with your coffee," he said; he was now growing very tired, folded his arms on the table, rested his head on them, yawned and said, "But now tell me a little about you."

The fireman had a gaunt face with blond stubble; he was about ten years younger than me, in his mid-twenties, and he had slightly discolored but good teeth.

"You have good teeth," I said.

"That's nice," the fireman said yawning, and then fell asleep.

"I know all about teeth," I said to the sleeping fireman, and suddenly Blank appeared in the kitchen door, rubbed his eyes, said, "Oh, a visitor. Sorry," and wanted to leave.

"Please stay."

Blank stopped and cleared his throat. "That, I believe, is the first guest you've had since we met each other," he said solemnly, looking at the sleeping fireman.

Blank was right, there had not been anyone here in a long time.

Evelyn's cruise dragged on; off the coast of Iceland there had been an engine failure, so Evelyn and the psychiatrist had prolonged the inevitable shore leave, and finally the repaired cruise ship had sailed off without them. Evelyn wrote me many postcards and I wondered whether the psychiatrist had written his patients to tell them he would be staying away longer, or whether the patients would be standing on the pier with welcoming flowers in hand on the day of his scheduled return and had been waiting for the psychiatrist; I imagined how the patients had been standing for hours in vain and looking out to sea, full of anticipation, then increasingly more apprehensive, and how finally, speechless and with tears in their eyes, they had pressed the flowers into the hands of someone who just happened by.

"That is not a guest," I said. "That is a fireman. He was looking for a fire. With a flashlight."

"That was obviously tiring," Blank said.

"Did you sleep well?"

"Wonderfully," he said. "And you? Have you slept at all?"

"No, but now I know all about a karate movie."

"That doesn't help," Blank said. "Eating something—that would help. Maybe you'd like to eat something now?"

"No, thank you."

"What are the choices?"

"Marzipan."

"Nothing else? Didn't you go shopping?"

"Nothing else."

Blank took a new bag of marzipan out of the cupboard.

"Thanks. I really don't want anything," I said.

"I know," said Blank. "I'll leave it out just in case. When your guest wakes up, he'll be hungry."

It was now early morning, and it was quiet. All you could hear was the fireman's soft snoring and the crackling sound of the marzipan bag in Blank's hands.

"I'm very glad you're here, Blank," I said.

Blank filled a bowl with the marzipan; he concentrated on that and did not look at me, but I could see that he was smiling. He set the bowl on the table. "It smells so different," he said. "Somehow fresher."

"Axe Shock musk oil," I said.

Blank looked at the fireman for a while, nodded at me and then left.

Half an hour later the fireman slowly lifted his head and blinked. "You slept," I said. "And how," he said, taking a handful of marzipan. "But now I have to go."

"Do you feel okay?"

"Sure, I feel fine."

"Are you sure?"

"I feel super," said the fireman, and stood up. "Don't give it a second thought."

On the way to the kitchen door he stood in front of the dresser that he could easily imagine in light green, and looked at the tea kettle. "Is that from the middle ages?"

I shook my head.

"The coil will burn right through that if you so much as look at it," the fireman said, and looked at the tea kettle, as if to prove it. "Always good to pull out the plug."

"I understand," I said.

I took him to the door. He walked in front of me, and he was so steady as he walked to the door, I did not believe there would be any side effects.

"Maybe we'll meet again," he said. He looked as if he wanted to say something and did not know exactly what and so, instead of saying something, he raised his eyebrows again. I raised my eyebrows, too.

"Maybe when there's really something burning," he finally said.

"For example," I said. The fireman nodded and left.

Blank asked me every two hours if I had eaten anything, and since I almost always said no, he thought up ruses. "You're much too thin; you need something to eat," he said. "We need to distract you. We have to do it in such a way that you don't realize you're eating."

Blank routinely made me a dish of the chicken fricassee that he had always cooked for his wife. Then he started a diversionary tactic. He read to me out loud anything at hand—a book, a newspaper, the text on a bag of marzipan—and he read everything out loud with great verve; in order to outwit me especially well, he read excerpts from the book by Evelyn's psychiatrist with just as much spirit as he read out the expiration date and the list of ingredients in the marzipan. He placed himself on a kitchen chair while I sat in front of the fricassee, and recited passages from famous speeches from Cicero, first in Latin, then in German, and at the same time made sweeping gestures.

"Don't fall down," I said.

Blank played *Sailor, Your Home is the Sea* on the out-of-tune accordion that had belonged to Jacob's grandmother; he sang it with tears in his eyes, several times in a row.

"Could you play something else?" I asked. "My repertoire is limited," Blank said, "I only know two pieces."

"What's the other one?"

Blank looked at me with embarrassment. "*Boy, Come Back Soon,*" I said. Blank nodded.

Nothing worked; in the end Blank ate every chicken fricassee himself after it had grown cold, even though he wasn't hungry, and only so it did not go bad. "Then just astronaut food," he finally said.

"Good idea," I said. I took out my wallet; there were only coins inside—there was nothing else. "There's hardly any money left," I said. There had hardly been any money left for some time, but now suddenly I could no longer deny it. Suddenly I could no longer deny all the overdue notices that dropped through the mail slot from time to time; I had placed them on the small table in the hallway and did not look at them again. Instead of looking I had expected the absurd: that eventually everyone would simply stop sending bills, courteously, because people don't like to be pushy. Blank patted the pockets of his suit. "Unfortunately, I don't have anything on me."

To do something about the silence that now set in and was interrupted only by an imaginary rustling of overdue notices in the hallway, I said: "Blank is Blank," and hoped that he would laugh, but of course he did not laugh.

"Will you actually inherit anything?" he asked.

"Definitely," I said. "I haven't been worried about it."

Blank cleared his throat. "And where is your husband's wallet?"

I picked up the bag from the hospital that was lying on top of the overdue notices. The wallet was inside, the bottle of *Tears Again*, and nothing else. They had not been able to give me Jacob's clothes. They had, the doctor had said apologetically, had to cut Jacob's clothes away from his body after the accident.

"Here," I said and put Jacob's wallet on the kitchen table. "Should I?" Blank asked. I nodded. He opened Jacob's wallet and bent over it like a watchmaker. He laid everything he found out on the table. I was anticipating the obvious. The obvious was bad; obvious was a receipt for a hotel room we had not been in together; a receipt for a gift that had not been for me; a sales slip from the drugstore, which, in addition to shower gel and deodorant, listed the item "condoms." Blank did not find the obvious. What he found was just as bad, because you couldn't imagine anything, and when you can't imagine anything, you can easily imagine the worst. Beside twelve dollars and seventy cents and Jacob's license and credit cards Blank placed a piece from a beer coaster on the table, on which someone had scrawled something indecipherable, and a torn-out, folded review of a Swedish film that Jacob had never mentioned. All that could mean everything and nothing; I could not imagine what it all meant, and began to imagine the worst things possible: along with the scrawled writing, along with the Swedish film, along with Jacob. Blank looked at me and tapped his index finger on the ATM card.

First I tried Jacob's birthday, and then mine. Both were wrong. "One more try," I said to Blank, and I was suddenly afraid that Jacob's secret code would be Alina's birthday, or the day he had met her. "I think it highly improbable that someone would change his pin number to the birthday of his beloved," Blank said.

"Probably not many," I said.

"Is that something Jacob would do?"

"I don't know what Jacob would do."

"Try your anniversary," Blank said.

I entered the date of our anniversary. The screen changed colors, choices appeared, and suddenly I was as excited as someone who goes into a casino for the first time. I turned to Blank. "What do you think? How much do we need?"

"A lot, I'd suggest," Blank said. "A whole lot, to start."

I was embarrassed to ask the pharmacist for astronaut food. I am always embarrassed to ask pharmacists for anything that is not clearly intended for use in external emergencies.

The pharmacist was wearing a sweater that was decorated with a screensaver from the nineties. "Hello," he said. "Can I help you?"

"I'd like a package of bandages," I said.

"Bandages with heat, bandages for blisters, or bandages for wounds?"

"For wounds, please."

The pharmacist took out the bandages. "For minor injuries. Extra strong adhesive."

"Thanks," I said. "Oh, and I also need astronaut food."

"A nutritional liquid supplement," the pharmacist corrected. "The type recommended after major surgery."

"Exactly."

"I only have the nut flavor in stock," the pharmacist said and took out a carton with four bottles that looked like beer. "This is highly caloric," he said, as if he was saying it was "highly explosive."

I brought the highly caloric carton home. "Would you like to try some?" I asked and poured Blank a glass. Blank tried it; you could tell that he didn't like it at all, but he smiled and said: "It doesn't taste bad. Is it vanilla?"

In the evening Blank and I sat on the balcony; I filled out bank transfer slips and drank the nutritional liquid supplement. Blank had bought a beer for himself; he drank it for no particular reason—Blank needed no fluid; Blank's body didn't need anything; I kept forgetting that.

That Blank, to be precise, was no longer alive, was so absurd that it did not surprise me. Blank exhibited all the signs of life. He breathed and spoke and swallowed and moved and his heart beat like someone who was alive. His heart, said Blank, was a Cor mobile.

"What's that?"

"Something quite rare," said Blank. "A Cor mobile is a so-called abnormal, movable heart; it wanders around in the chest. You have to clamp it in place surgically."

Because it was dim and Blank and I could barely see each other, I asked him if he had died because of his movable heart. My own heart was beating fast because I had never asked anyone what they had died of; I had not expected I would ever ask someone that. No place in the world, I had believed, could be so pitch black that I would have asked someone there what they had died of.

"No," Blank said, "that won't kill you." He loosened his tie. "It was a heart attack," he said, then nodded, as if he had asked himself what he had died of.

I didn't know how I should respond, whether it would be appropriate to say, "You have my deepest sympathy" the way you would to the bereaved; I didn't know whether Blank was his own bereaved, and whether, now that he was no longer alive, he found it sad to have died; or whether he found it sad to have died of a heart attack; after all, a heart attack was probably a little better than a car accident, a bolt of lightning, or a killer; I didn't know whether a dead man cares at all about the cause of his death or whether it was as important as the fact that one came into the world by Caesarean section or by traditional childbirth was for the living.

"But I'm feeling pretty good now," Blank said.

I looked at Blank's chest and imagined his movable heart as it wandered around in his chest, as if it had been spooked while sleepwalking; I imagined how his heart in its wanderings was always nudged somewhere, its rhythm slightly disturbed by fear, and then had taken a different direction, unremittingly, until someone had resolved to clamp it; I wondered whether Blank's heart would have endured longer and would have later stopped if it had not been clamped.

"Now is it ... is it like it was before? Your body, I mean."

Blank looked down at himself. "No," he said. "I can feel everything, but it's strangely muted, as if I'm always wearing a diving suit. It's as if I were filled with air. I feel, on the whole, too light."

"Stand up, please," I said and went over to Blank. Blank rose. "May I?" I asked. Blank nodded; I wrapped my arms around his waist and tried to lift him up, I tried it several times, but he was too heavy. "You're too heavy," I said, and Blank rejoiced. "I weighed about two hundred pounds," he said. I looked at Blank with astonishment, his large, very thin body in the black suit. Blank smiled. "I have very heavy bones."

The doorbell rang. I didn't move; Blank looked at me. "I'm not expecting anybody," I said. "For all I care, it would be fine if you open it," Blank said. It rang again. "We still have time," I said, and tried not to make it sound like a question. "Yes," Blank said, "we still have time."

The fireman stood in front of the door. "I'd like to have another cup of that coffee," he said. He patted his uniform, as if it was covered with dust.

"What's your name?"

"Armin. Armin Golling."

I leaned against the door frame. "Unfortunately, there isn't any more coffee, Armin," I said. "Not that particular variety, anyway."

"Too bad." Armin looked past me into the apartment.

"Do you have company?"

"No."

"May I come in? Just for a minute?"

I looked at him quizzically. "I just put out a fire in the

neighborhood," he explained.

When I opened the door completely Armin went into the kitchen, sat down and stretched out his legs. I thought about my aunt and the postman on his daily route who always made a stop at my aunt's place. She always kept a sweet liqueur ready for him, and while the postman drank his sweet liqueur, he and my aunt talked about the latest news from the neighborhood. For my aunt, who had no one to talk to, it was the high point of the day. Armin sat at my kitchen table as if he had been coming regularly for many years, as if what Armin was doing was so common that he was the high point of the day and as if I was always on the lookout for him and kept a sweet liqueur ready.

"I can't offer you anything," I said. "Just marzipan. And a high-calorie nutritional liquid supplement."

"High-calorie sounds good."

"High-calorie," I repeated. "Not high percentage."

I put a bottle on the table. The bottle of astronaut food had a crown cap; I quickly took the bottle opener from the balcony, because I was afraid Armin would otherwise open the bottle with his teeth. Blank was no longer on the balcony. I put the opener on the table and said: "I have to go to the bathroom for a minute."

I found Blank in the living room; he was standing at the window, his hands folded behind his back, and looking into the garden. When I walked in, he turned and smiled. "Another fire alarm?"

"No," I said. "Don't you want to sit down?"

"Maybe later," Blank said. I went back into the kitchen. "It tastes just great," Armin said and put the half-empty bottle on the table.

"Five hundred calories per bottle," I said, "if you drink three of them a day, you'll gain twelve pounds in two weeks."

"It's worth it," Armin said. "Do you want some?"

"That was the last."

"It would be even better with ice," Armin said, got up, took a knife out of the drawer, opened the fridge, hacked some ice from the icy freezer and pushed it into the bottle.

"Well," Armin asked, "are you okay?"

"Yes. But I'm a bit tired."

"Long day?"

"Yes."

"Me too."

We were silent; Armin leaned back; the leaf of the potted palm, which had settled on his head the last time, settled there again.

"Did you feel funny after you were here last time?" I asked. "Afterwards, did something peculiar happen to you?"

"No," said Armin. "To you?"

"No."

"Have you seen the movie? The one with Ralph McQuincey? The one I was telling you about?"

"No," I said. "You were just here the day before yesterday." Because Armin looked very disappointed, I said: "My TV is broken."

"I see," he said. "I'll bring my computer with me next time."

"I have to go to the toilet again," I said.

I went into the bedroom. Blank was in bed, flipping through the book by Evelyn's psychiatrist. Since the night after the funeral Blank had slept in Jacob's and my bed, which was now just my bed, and I slept on the sofa in the living room. I had persuaded him. "It's very uncomfortable to me, to monopolize your bed," Blank said. I said that someone else entirely had monopolized my bed and that I would much rather sleep on the sofa.

"I already lay down," Blank said now. "I don't want be rude; next time I'll certainly introduce myself. I'm just so tired tonight."

"Don't you feel well? Are you sick?"

"No," he said. "Luckily, I can no longer get sick."

"Of course," I said. "Sorry."

"And I feel very well," he said and smiled.

"What's it going to be? Another karate movie?"

"Likely soon."

"We should see one sometime," Blank said, "I'm not familiar with a single one."

"Okay," I said. Blank put the book on the bedside table.

"Good night," he said and patted me on the forearm.

"Good night, Blank," I said.

"Diarrhea?" Armin asked. He had pushed his chair further away from the table and was now very close to the re-glued flamingo. I pushed the flamingo to the side, leaned against the sink, folded my arms and definitely wanted to avoid talking about a karate movie. "Do you know what a Cor mobile is?"

Armin also crossed his arms. "I dunno. Something to do with a glee club?"

I rolled my eyes and took a glass from the cupboard. "A wandering heart," Armin said behind my back. "Extremely rare. An abnormal, moveable heart, that wanders around in the chest."

I turned around. "Got you," he said.

Armin grinned, stood up slowly, unbuttoned his jacket and then his shirt, slowly, like a stripper for a bachelorette party disguised as a fireman.

"What's this all about?" I asked, "Are you crazy?"

"Don't worry. I just want to show you something." Armin kept his shirt on. Across his chest there was a tattoo, one sentence in a sweeping, ornate script that tilted to the right: *Nothing is forever*.

I burst out laughing. Armin looked at me blankly. "Actually, that wasn't especially funny," he said. Vertically across his chest there was a pale scar. "Sorry," I said.

"I didn't see that; the tattoo is so ... distracting."

"There was something wrong with my heart when I was a child," said Armin. "Since then I know all about heart disease. You can ask me anything about it, any time."

I went closer to Armin and looked at the tattoo. It had an incredible number of embellishments, and up close it looked as if the tattooist had embellished so much because he had initially devoted himself to the "t" and the "h". The *Nothing* looked like a corrected *Nofking*.

"Everything's been okay for a long time," Armin said. "Thanks for asking."

He pressed his chin to his chest, looked at the tattoo as if he was seeing it for the first time, and then nodded appreciatively.

"Nothing is forever," he said solemnly. "That's how it is. Ralph McQuincey, incidentally, has the same one, in exactly the same spot."

Armin settled in. He came by every other day; he had always just allegedly done something in the vicinity: rescued a cat from a tree, removed a layer of diesel fuel, explained something about fire safety to school children, responded to a false alarm.

"Are you actually a real fireman?"

"Sure," said Armin. I did not believe Armin was a fireman; his uniform looked like it came from a costume shop. "As surely as I'm standing here," he said.

I did not tell him that standing there was not always an argument. "Your uniform looks kind of like a costume," I said, thinking of a bachelorette party.

"How many firemen have you seen up close?"

"None," I admitted.

I began to expect Armin, in the same way I had expected Jacob's spontaneous aunt. I would open the door and wave him in without saying a word; Armin would walk past me into the kitchen, sit down, stay for two hours and leave again. Blank never got around to it; Blank was always indisposed, he was always just too tired or was taking a walk. "You really can come," I said. "I know," said Blank. Armin would explain the climatic scenes from movies with Ralph McQuincey, and to make him stop I would say that it was a shame if he gave everything away.

Because Armin offered again and again to bring his computer along with him the next time, I insisted that everything still looked blurry. This was not true. I could see everything all right now, every wrinkle in Blank's face was crystal clear, all the furniture, all the door jambs; recently nothing got jostled anymore; recently, all distances were estimated just right.

After Armin had recounted everything about his karate film actor, about rescues from basements and his grandfather's pig breeding, about previous girlfriends he had been forced to leave because they always wanted more than he was willing to give, he would ask me how things were going for me. When Armin brought along a bottle of champagne, I got pretty drunk on one glass and then drank more, and I told him about Jacob. Because of the champagne everything was spinning and I mixed everything up, about Jacob and Alina and Jacob and me, and Jacob and the accident, and always, when I arrived at a climactic moment, it occurred to me that I had forgotten to explain something which you had to know to understand the climax, and then after each respective climax I explained what made the climax a climax.

When I got to the end of everything, Armin puffed his cheeks out. "Sad story."

"Yes," I said, rested my head on the table and fell asleep.

When I woke up, it was dawn. Armin was sitting opposite me and smiled. "You slept," he said.

"And how," I said, "but now you have to leave again."

Armin stood up, filled two tall glasses with tap water and placed one in front of me. "Did you still have sex, when he was with the other woman?"

"What?" I asked. I asked it like an aunt with a sweet liquor.

"Did you still have sex, when he was with the other woman?"

I could not remember the last time.

"I can't remember the last time," I said, and Armin said: "Then it probably wasn't that great."

"No, of course I can remember having sex with Jacob," I said. "I just can't remember when the last time was," and Armin said: "Then it probably wasn't that great."

I took Armin's almost empty bottle of nutritional liquid supplement from the table, put it on the sink and arranged myself in front of him. "Why are you really always coming here?"

"Because I'm in the neighborhood."

"That's nonsense."

Armin leaned back. "I am always coming here because I believe that you need company. Nobody comes here, except me. If anybody did come here, you'd wash yourself once in a while. Or take out the garbage."

I sat down on the kitchen chair. "I think you come here because *you* need company," I said. "I have company already, and the best that you can imagine."

"Oh?"

"I'm not alone. I've always wanted to tell you that."

"Oh? And where is he? A business trip? Longer than expected." Armin retrieved the nutritional liquid supplement from the sink, stood in front of the table and emptied the bottle. Whenever he came, he drank about two bottles. I looked at his belly, the uniform stretched over it. He had put on weight.

I got up, went into Blank's room and shook his shoulder. "Blank, you really have to come in now," I said.

I pushed Blank into the kitchen. Armin crossed his hands behind his neck and looked at me. Blank stood there like an oversized candidate for confirmation who has slept through the repeated lessons.

"Dr. Blank, this is Armin," I said. "Armin, this is Doctor Friedrich Blank."

Armin looked at me, and then in the direction I had pointed.

"I'm glad to meet you," Blank said.

Then no one said anything, so I said, "Nice that you two finally get to meet each other."

"I think so too," said Blank. "Until now, I was unfortunately always indisposed."

Armin got up, walked around the kitchen table to Blank and me and took me aside, as if he was planning a confidential business meeting.

"But you do realize that there is no one there," he whispered, and he whispered it specifically not like a question.

"You see," Blank said to me, "I was afraid of that."

"Dr. Friedrich Blank, a classicist," I said to Armin. "As surely as I'm standing here."

Armin went back around the kitchen table, sat down in his seat and looked between me and the place where Blank was standing, back and forth. Armin looked like a quiz show contestant on TV who thinks exceedingly ardently over an exceedingly valuable question.

'As surely I'm standing here," I said. "And as surely as your grandfather is a pig breeder. And all the more, as surely as you are a fireman."

Armin looked at me for a long time. Then he raised his arms and leaned back like a quiz show contestant who has decided to swap the question.

"Okay," he said. "Dr. Friedrich Blank." He raised his nutritional liquid supplement in Blank's direction. "A special toast to you."

When Armin dropped by the next time, he was in civilian clothes and had a travel bag as well, and he did go not directly to the kitchen, but remained standing in the hallway. "Your boss told you that you should go on vacation," he said, "so go on vacation. You need to get away from here badly."

"With you?" I asked. "With me," Armin said, as if he were the proud owner of an entire cruise ship fleet.

"I can't afford to take a vacation," I said.

"Neither can I," Armin said. "So Holland is just the right place."

"Holland?"

"Yes. Zandvoort. A romantic seaside resort with a lot of options, even on a small budget. I have something to do there. Something important." Armin looked diagonally past me. "Doctor Blank? What do you think? Is a vacation a good idea?"

"Blank is in the bedroom," I said. "And how is that going to work, the three of us, when you can't even communicate with Blank."

"You're a translator," Armin said. Blank came out of the bedroom. "Armin is going to Holland," I said, "and wants us to go with him."

"An excellent idea," Blank said. "You need to get away from here badly."

Armin looked at me expectantly. "So?"

I thought of Bengt, who had indeed wanted me not only to take a vacation, but also to be more creative with my translations.

"Blank has strong doubts," I said to Armin.

"You have misunderstood me there," Blank said.

Armin rolled his eyes. "Come on. Think it over."

"Well, I'll think it over," I said, so Armin would leave and I would not feel bad about not going with him. "Write down your number for me."

"You know my number already," Armin said. "Everybody knows my number." I raised my eyebrows.

"911," Armin said.

He sat on his travel bag. "Come on, think it over now," he said, raising a finger in the air. "*Always think for yourself and constantly try new things.*"

"That's from a famous inscription in a 17th Century church," Blank said.

"Karate rule number twenty," Armin said.

"Oh," said Blank.

"Holland isn't anything new," I said.

"That's a bit of a lame excuse," Blank said.

"But I am," Armin said.

"But Blank, there was also something you had to take care of," I said. "You've got that appointment."

"That can wait."

I looked at the place where Jacob's sign had stood, *Soon it will be over*; I had carried it to the basement, but it was always still there. Everything was always still there.

"But I'll have to call someone about the houseplant," I said, even though the houseplant was a palm tree that didn't need anything, and even though I didn't know anyone I could call to look after it. Blank nodded at me forcefully as if I had said: "Maybe I'll have a bit of that chicken fricassee."

Tonight It's Very Clear

We took my car. I drove; Armin was sitting next to me and Blank was in the back seat. He sat right in the middle and he had both windows open, his hair fluttering in the wind. *Just* was written in large gold letters on the rear window behind him. The *Married* was vaguely perceptible. After the wedding Jacob and I had tried everything possible to clean the rear window, but when the *Married* would not come off after an hour, we gave up.

"Music?" Armin asked and turned on the radio. Then he turned to Blank. "What's it really like when you die?"

"Armin!" I said, as if Armin was as a child in the waiting room who had asked his mother out loud why the uncle on the chair beside her was so fat. I looked in the rearview mirror; Blank didn't bat an eyelash. "I'll tell you later," he said.

Armin looked at me. "So?"

"Wait a while," I said.

Armin turned back to Blank. "What kind of appointment did you have?"

"I need to go see my wife," Blank said.

I looked at Blank in the rearview mirror. "A private appointment," I said to Armin. "With his wife, if you really have to know."

"Is your wife also dead?" Armin asked.

"No," said Blank. "She's still alive."

I shook my head.

"But getting a bit long in the tooth, right?"

"Sixty-two now, soon," said Blank, "On the eighth of March."

The radio host announced a new song; Armin turned around and stared at the radio. "*Karate Kid II*," he exclaimed. "The title track," and turned it up louder. "What?" I asked. "The title song," Armin said with excitement. "I can't understand the lyrics. Can you translate it?"

"What?"

"Translate it!"

"I can't listen and translate at the same time."

"Here we go," Armin yelled. "Go ahead!"

The song began; it was accompanied by an orchestra.

"'Tonight it's very clear,' he's singing," I translated. "'As we're both lying here,' he's singing now."

"You don't have to keep saying that he's singing. I know that already," Armin said.

"'There's so many things I want to say,'" I translated. "'I will always love you. I will never leave you.'"

Armin nodded. He looked at me expectantly.

"'Sometimes I just forget,'" I said, "'say things I might regret. It breaks my heart to see you crying. I don't wanna lose you. I could never make it alone.' Give me the water."

Armin handed me the bottle of water and hung on my every word.

"'I am the man who will fight for your honor,'" I said. "'I'll be the hero you're dreaming of. We'll live forever, knowing together that we did it all for the glory of love. You keep me standing still.'"

"'Keep me standing tall,'" Blank corrected behind me.

"'You help me through it all,'" I said. "'I'm always strong when you're beside me.'"

"Aha," Armin said.

"'I have always needed you,'" I said. "'I could never make it alone. I am the man who will fight for your honor, I'll be the hero you've been dreaming of, we'll live forever ...'"

"You don't have to keep repeating the chorus," Armin said.

"'We'll live forever,'" I said, "'knowing together that we did it all for the glory of love.'"

Blank had leaned forward and looked at me from the side.

"'Just like a knight in shining armor, from a long time ago,'" I said very loudly, "'I will ... what? ... I will save the day - or something like that - and take you to my castle far away. I am the man who will fight for your honor, I'll be the hero that you're dreaming of, we'll live forever, forever, knowing together that we did it all, absolutely everything, for the glory of love, for the glory of love.'" The singer did not stop stressing that, "for the glory of love, we did it all, did it all for the glory of love,'" I said, and then I burst into tears.

Blank patted me on the shoulder. Armin looked at me with disappointment. "I thought it was about karate," he said.

We stopped at a gas station. Armin went to the toilet. I was standing at a high table drinking coffee from the vending machine. Blank walked through the gas station and looked at the sale items, the bread rolls wrapped in plastic, energy drinks and yogurt, the magazines—women's magazines and porn and motor sports—the stuffed animals with fabric hearts on their feet that said *Mom*, or *I Love You*.

When Armin returned, Blank said: "We should buy supplies."

"Blank wants something to eat," I said, although Blank never needed to eat anything. Armin was suddenly in a hurry. "Let's go," he said, and pushed us out of the gas station.

"Step on the gas," he said when we got in the car. I drove off. Once we were on the highway Armin opened his bag; there were three yogurt drinks and three-wrapped sandwiches and several candy bars inside. "Where did you get all that?" I asked.

"Stolen."

"What?" I asked and in shock gave it so much gas we were forced back in our seats. "Careful," Blank cried, and clutched my head rest. "It's only bread," he said, "it wasn't a bank robbery."

"Why did you do that?" I asked. Armin bit into a chocolate bar.

"Just because," he said, chewing.

I drove faster than I had ever driven in my life. "Give me one," I said, reaching into Armin's pocket without taking my eyes off the road, pulled out a packaged roll and tore the foil off with my teeth.

"You have a few screws loose," I said with the foil between my teeth. "Calm down," Armin said.

I spit the foil into the footwell and bit into the bun.

"You can let up on the gas," Blank said. "We're not in a getaway car."

"Sure," I said.

We arrived at night. For the rest of the trip, Armin had repeated the plots from Ralph McQuincey's karate movies. Armin had chosen the guesthouse *De Vrolijke Herder*. Everywhere in the narrow hallway and in the reception area, pinned up with colorful tacks, hung huge photos of sunrises and sunsets, swaying, tall grass, glittering snowflakes on branches and rainbows over seas, and on each of the images there was a curled sentence that presumably said something contemplative. Right next to the entrance hung a large mirror, and above it were the words: *Here you see the person who is responsible for your life*. I looked in the mirror. Blank was standing behind me. "That's very kind of you," I said. Blank laughed. "You, too."

We had two single rooms. "Would you have an extra bed?" I asked the owner, who looked like Jacob's ancient, transparent grandmother. "There is one already there," she said. Armin grinned at me. "I thought of everything," he said.

There was also a rainbow photo hanging in the room I shared with Blank. The bathroom was across the hall. The bed was short, the extra bed even shorter. "Take the regular bed," I said, and Blank was too tired to say that it was uncomfortable for him and would prefer me to take the bed. "Thanks," he said, and lay down. I brushed my teeth and lay down on the bed. "It's fine to wake me," Blank said, "if there's anything." And then we fell asleep.

At three o'clock in the morning I woke up. I turned on the bedside lamp. Blank was fast asleep, his feet in the black patent leather shoes hanging over the edge of the bed. The light in the windowless hallway was broken. It flickered on briefly in irregular intervals, and then it was pitch black. I remembered that there were five doors in the hallway, but I no longer knew which one was the door to the toilet. Suddenly I heard a suppressed cough at the end of the hallway.

"Is anyone there?" I asked.

"Yes," whispered Armin and turned on his flashlight. "I'm here."

He was sitting in front of the last door, wearing nothing but striped pajama pants.

"What are you doing?"

"Come here," Armin said. I went to him; he pulled me by the arm down to him. I sat down beside him. Armin put his arm around me, pointed at the door in front of us and smiled, as if we were sitting on a sofa watching his favorite show. "What?" I asked.

"Not so loud," Armin whispered and waved his arms, "or you'll wake him up." Then he leaned back again and beamed at me. "He's in there," he whispered.

"Who?"

"Ralph McQuincey."

I woke up because Blank was running his fingers through my hair. "We're going to miss the breakfast," he said.

I sat up. "Three rooms down there is a karate movie star," I said. "Armin is sitting outside his door waiting for him to come out."

"Did you dream it?"

"No," I said. "He's probably still sitting there."

"But why would a karate movie star put up in a pension in Zandvoort?"

"I don't have the faintest idea," I said and got out of the bed. We went into the hall. Armin was still sitting there.

"Are you absolutely sure?" I asked Armin.

"A thousand percent," Armin said. "I've thoroughly researched it. He's in Zandvoort, he is in this hotel, and he is in this room."

"But why?" I asked.

"Because it's absurd," Armin said. "Because nobody comes here. Because he's not besieged by fans here."

"That doesn't really add up," Blank said.

"Don't look at me like that," Armin said to me. "I'm not a fan, I'm a disciple."

"Have you heard any sounds in there?" I asked.

"No."

"Knock a few times."

Armin looked at me aghast. "No! Maybe he's meditating."

"Come on," I said. "We're going to eat breakfast."

"I'm staying here," Armin said.

Armin continued to sit. He sat there in front of the door for three full days. We brought him pillows, drinks, food and a shirt; we tried to persuade him to come out for at least half an hour, but Armin said: "Then I might miss him. I have no idea how long he's going to stay. Maybe he'll only come out when he's ready to leave."

I put my ear to the door several times a day. You never heard anything. Once a day the owner came up to the corridor to vacuum; Armin lifted his legs; she vacuumed around Armin. I asked the owner if there was anyone staying in the room. She shook her head. "She has to say that," Armin said. "McQuincey is incognito."

Armin did not move from the door. During the day Blank and I walked along the sea, a few times because we wanted to, and a few other times because otherwise there was not much to do in Zandvoort; we estimated the distances incorrectly and came back late and we sat down in the hallway with Armin for every dinner.

On the third evening Blank and I did not return until ten. Armin drank a lot of beer and fell asleep, so there was no longer any reason to sit in the hallway. Blank folded up my empty aluminum pan, which had contained lasagna; Armin had not eaten his. I turned on the bedside lamp which we had put in the hallway for Armin. "Your wife," I said. "What is she really like?"

Blank tried to seal the cardboard lid on Armin's lasagna tray, but the lasagna could not be resealed again.

"Maybe you met her once," Blank said. "She has black curly hair, usually piled up. She never wears pants, always narrow skirts that hang just above the knee. In the winter she wears a half-length, camel hair coat. In the summer blouses, mostly with polka dots. She's not very large, rather small and a little chubby." He said it like someone at the police department who wants to report someone missing.

"I can't remember," I said. "What does she do?"

The light flickered briefly, and then went out again.

"She works at Schirms," Blank said, "a gentlemen's tailor in the city center." Blank wrapped Armin's tray in a plastic bag.

"My wife lives in your neighborhood." He looked at me. "Otherwise we probably never would have met."

I remembered the night when I first saw Blank, when I had scrubbed the bathroom and had tried to think of a country beginning with X. "What were you really doing in my hallway?"

"I just wanted to rest," Blank said. "The front door was ajar, and I was tired. Then I really just wanted to go straight to my wife."

"And then?"

Blank smiled. "Then you met me." He made a knot in the bag containing Armin's lasagna and was suddenly a little embarrassed. "You also looked tired. Very tired. And then I got the idea that ... that I could look after you a little. And you could look after me."

I grabbed Blank's hand, which he was now using to make a second knot in the bag. "A very good idea," I said.

The hall light flickered, and then went out again. "But why didn't we ever see each other if you lived in the neighborhood?"

"That's the way it is," Blank said. "Sometimes you just meet very late."

"And your wife? Weren't you afraid that we might suddenly encounter her?"

"No," said Blank. "I know when you can encounter her and where, and when you can't. I know my wife's timetable." He said it as if his wife was an astronomical event.

"How long were you married?"

Armin woke up and pointed at the door. "Have I missed anything?"

"No," I said.

"Thirty-six years," Blank said.

"That's longer than I've lived," I said.

Armin rubbed his eyes. "What's longer than you've lived?"

"Blank's marriage."

"Oh," said Armin. "And? Was it a happy marriage?"

Blank stared at his palms. "She cheated on me quite often," he said. Armin looked at me. "It's okay for him to hear it," Blank said.

"She cheated on him," I explained.

"With who?" Armin asked. Blank put the bag with the lasagna on the floor, exhaled as if he had held his breath for a long time, and made a waving gesture. "With the gentlemen's tailor, with the gentlemen's tailor's customers, with the son of one of the gentlemen's tailor's customers, and with one of my students."

Blank had worked as a lecturer at the university; he had taught students intermediate and advanced Latin, I explained to Armin. "Some were truly gifted," Blank said and I added, "some delivered very beautiful translations."

"Recite a beautiful translation for me," Armin said.

Blank sat up. "I believe we must now say something important about the value and benefits of the province." I repeated it and tried to say it with the same emotion as Blank.

"What's so beautiful about that?" Armin asked and Blank said, "That's what my wife always asked."

"How do you know who she cheated with?" Armin asked. "Did she tell you that?"

The light flickered in the hall. "Partly," Blank said. "Once, I also searched through her desk. There I stumbled on the letters, which, in terms of their clarity, didn't leave much to be desired. Instead, they left nothing to hope for."

"Blank found letters," I said.

"When someone finds letters, they've looked for them before," Armin said.

"Yes," Blank said. "You begin, in such situations, to do things that you never thought you would ever do."

The lights flickered.

"I'd flip out," Armin said, "if someone cheated on me; I would flip out." He said this to me as if we were negotiating the basic rules of our marriage. "And what did you do with the letters?" he asked. "Translate them into Latin, or what?"

Blank said nothing. "Why didn't you leave?" Armin asked.

Blank pointed to the door. "Why don't you just go away?"

"Because he loved her, you idiot," I said.

"True," said Blank, "but that's not always a good argument."

Then suddenly it grew very bright. It grew bright because the room door, which Armin had been sitting in front of for days, was opened. I squinted. In the door frame appeared a man who was very large, quite fat and blond. He wore nothing but a T-shirt and boxer shorts. Armin jumped up. "Dear Mr. McQuincey," he said in English. "I was waiting for you. I was waiting for you three days and three nights." It was evident that Armin had learned this text by heart and now only had to use the correct number.

"I arrived this morning," said Mr. McQuincey. "You were sleeping."

Blank and I stood up. "My name is Armin Golling, and here is friends," Armin said. He was trembling with excitement. "Here is Katja Wiesberg." The light flickered in the hall again. "She is nice girl, but she have ... she have Wackelkontakt with Realität." Armin poked me in the side. "What does Wackelkontakt mean? And Realität?"

"Intermittent contact," I said, shaking McQuincey's hand. "Intermittent contact with reality."

"And here," Armin pointed in Blank's direction, "here is Dr. Friedrich Blank. No matter not to see."

Mr. McQuincey's face was puffy and blotchy red; he raised his eyebrows, looked from one to the other and then a long time at the point where Blank was standing. "Nice to meet you," he said.

His breath reeked of alcohol.

"So," Armin said, "we swim?"

Mr. McQuincey looked at his wristwatch. "It's the middle of the night," he said, and belched. "Sorry."

"Yes," Armin said and made breaststroke motions. "We swim?"

McQuincey took a deep breath; I was standing directly in front of him and held my breath as he exhaled. He leaned on the door frame with one arm, rested his head on his upper arm and deliberated. His face was close to his armpit. McQuincey sniffed.

"Okay," McQuincey said. "Why not? Why not go swimming?"

We walked to the beach. Armin and Mr. McQuincey walked a few feet in front of me and Blank. McQuincey carried a rolled towel under his arm. He had not put on anything else except flip-flops; it was much too cold for a t-shirt and boxer shorts, but McQuincey did not look like he was cold. He looked like he had never, ever been cold. Armin had the bag with the remains of his lasagna in his hand and he was carried away; he talked excitedly and gesticulated wildly at McQuincey. Because they were far ahead we could not understand much, and McQuincey probably didn't understand much either. Now and then Armin turned around and called out a word to me, and then I called back the translation: "Amazing," I cried; "unbeatable," "brilliant," "great," "supernatural," and "seven times." McQuincey listened to Armin, nodded and did not say much. Sometimes you could hear him laugh out loud or say a single sentence—he had a very loud voice.

"You've really seen that one?" he asked repeatedly. "Yes, that was back in the seventies," he said once; "Good gracious - you really remember that?" he asked, laughing uproariously. Blank walked by my side through the sand in his patent leather shoes. While making one of his gestures the bag with the lasagna had fallen from Armin's hand, but he was too excited to notice it; I picked up the bag. "Now he's very happy," I said to Blank.

"Yes," said Blank. "I think Mr. McQuincey has not been admired that much in a long time."

We laid our towels on the sand near the shore. It was after midnight, there was nobody here but us; the night was cloudless and the moon almost full. I pulled my shoes off; the sand was rough and cold and it would easily keep anyone awake.

"Show me, please," Armin said and sat down on his towel. McQuincey hesitated. He said he did not know if he could still do it, it had been a long time ago, and besides, he said, he had never really learned properly.

"He's a bit out of practice," I explained.

"Oh, no matter," said Armin.

Blank and I sat next to Armin. McQuincey took his position in front of the sea. He hopped up and down; his stomach and his cheeks shook. Then he leaned forward, bent one leg, spread one arm out, stood quite unbalanced, and looked like a stocky duck pretending it wanted to be a flamingo.

I remembered a dermatologist I had gone to see when I was twenty years old, to get a prescription for something reliable that would get rid of pimples. Because of puberty, I had grown a bit chubby and asked the dermatologist how to lose weight in a healthy way. The dermatologist had looked me over from top to bottom. "Don't even try," she had then said. "You can't make a Greyhound out of a Saint Bernard."

McQuincey briefly remained in his flamingo position, and then he fell over. "I definitely drank too much tonight," he said.

"He has to warm up," I said.

Armin nodded with understanding. McQuincey stood up, shook his arms and legs and took a few deep breaths. Then he leaped amazingly high and kicked the air with his right leg out. Armin clapped wildly, and from sheer surprise at his high jump McQuincey clapped along with him. Then he made movements with his arms that looked as if he wanted to scare away someone you could not see; he lunged forward, jumped up again, stumbled and fell on his butt.

We applauded. McQuincey wiped the sweat from his forehead.

"I would like to do that, too," Blank said, standing up.

"Mr. Blank would like to do that, too," I said.

McQuincey looked at me in astonishment. "Mr. Blank?" I nodded.

McQuincey beat his forehead. "Oh, of course," he said. "Mr. Blank," and pointed out that that he could not see Blank; he looked at Armin and pointed to his eyes with his index and middle finger and shrugged.

"The greatest fights are against the enemies that we cannot see, my son," Armin said and gave me a pleading look for help. I translated it as best we could.

"You say that in *Storms of Thunder*," Armin said. McQuincey laughed out loud. "You've seen that?" he asked and then looked at a spot just beside me. "Okay then, Mr. Blank."

"He's right in front of you," I said.

McQuincey put one foot forward, stretched out both hands in Blank's direction and began to circle him. Blank took the same pose and circled McQuincey. Sometimes McQuincey made a quick step forward, and then Blank backed away. McQuincey let out a choppy, roaring sound, like the noise my father had once made during sports events on television. "It's a battle cry," Armin said. Armin and I sat side by side in the sand; I watched as Blank in his suit and McQuincey in his boxer shorts circled each other. Armin looked at me; he made a movement as if he wanted to stretch and then put an arm around me. Because McQuincey often made a quick step forward and Blank avoided him, they slowly spun off to the right. Armin grabbed my ponytail and wound it around his hand. My head tilted backwards. Armin smiled; I unwound his hand from my hair and placed it on his leg. McQuincey jumped high into the air and kicked and Blank did the same; both fell, Blank laughed loudly, McQuincey roared with laughter, banged his fist into the sand and grinned in Blank's direction. "You hit me," he cried.

McQuincey got up and ran towards the sea, while running he pulled off his T-shirt, circled it a few times over his head and then threw it behind him. Armin undressed quickly and ran after him.

Blank stood a little distance away from me and looked at the water. For a moment he was undecided, and then he pulled off his shoes, socks, and pants. You could tell that he had not done all this in a very long time. He took off his jacket, unbuttoned his shirt and pulled his undershirt over his head. He put everything together neatly, and then took off his glasses. Except for his white underwear Blank was now naked and spindly. The long scar running vertically across his chest looked fresh.

Blank looked down at himself. He looked at himself as if what he saw was not his body, but an average quality translation from Latin. He glanced over at me. Then he ran into the sea.

McQuincey, out of the water, let out a scream and pointed at Armin's chest, embraced Armin firmly and then lifted him up. Blank ran with large strides towards the two of them, jumped up and down in the water and then plunged headlong into it, then reappeared; I heard him laugh and snort. I unwrapped Armin's lasagna and ate it; McQuincey lifted Armin into the air again and threw him into the water; Armin hooted, scrambled to his feet and lunged at McQuincey; Blank fell repeatedly backward into the water, reappeared, and beckoned to me with both arms; I waved back and found that all of this spoke explicitly against a secret plan to follow my husband in death and for getting on with my life. I took out my cell phone; it was in my jacket pocket, along with Jacob's vial of *Tears Again*. The phone lit up when I flipped it open, and I was pleased that the first person I wanted to tell that the time I felt my life had stopped was over, was not Jacob.

"Were you asleep?" I asked Evelyn. "No," she said. "How are you?"

"Evelyn," I said, "you won't believe it. I'm at the beach with a fireman, who, I think, is not really a fireman, a drunken karate movie star and a dead classical scholar. Right now they're all swimming."

Evelyn didn't say anything, and then: "Should I come home?"

"Evelyn," I said. I was laughing, and then suddenly I had to cry.

"Evelyn, it's beautiful here. Did I ever tell you about the dermatologist?"

"I'm afraid not."

I told Evelyn what the dermatologist had said about me and Greyhounds and Saint Bernards twenty years ago.

"Impudence," said Evelyn.

"I drive by her place sometimes," I said. "I'll tell her how it is. She'll be very surprised."

"Is everything really okay?"

"Yes," I said. "What about you?"

"Everything is fine with me," said Evelyn. "There's only one thing I miss."

"Me."

"Marzipan. Promise me you won't eat it all. Now that I'm with the psychiatrist, nobody gives it to me anymore. At least not in Iceland. Do you know what I'm doing right now?"

"Watching a volcano eruption."

"I'm in the hotel, and I'm translating."

"In Iceland?"

"Bengt can find me anywhere."

"Bengt," I said, "Bengt. What kind of name is that? I'll surprise him, too. And his stupid new English translator, too."

"You're ready for a fight, aren't you?" Evelyn asked. "And what was all that just now about the karate star and the fireman? Who are swimming?"

"I need to hang up," I said. "Are you coming back soon?"

Blank came out of the water, with Armin and McQuincey on either side. They actually had almost exactly the same tattoo in exactly the same spot, even if McQuincey's was less ornate.

McQuincey plopped down in the sand, took his towel and began drying himself, giving special attention between the toes. Armin stood beside me and dripped. "Is everything okay?" he asked me and ruffled my hair. "Yes," I said looking up into the cloudless sky. "Tonight it's very clear." Armin kissed me on the head and ran away. "I'll run myself dry," he shouted over his shoulder.

Blank had stopped a few steps away from us. He raised his shoulders and wrapped his arms around his upper body. His hair glinted with water droplets.

I held Armin's towel out to him. He shook his head.

I stood up. "What is it?" I asked. Blank trembled. At first I thought he was just cold, and then I realized he was crying.

"Blank," I said, putting my hand gently on his shoulder. He winced; I took my hand away. Blank clapped his hands over his face.

"I miss all of this," he said. "You can't believe how much I miss all of this, and I especially miss all that I always missed—the sea, for instance," Blank said between his hands, and now his whole body was shivering. I've never been to the sea enough, you understand, and I also miss what I've never known—karate, for instance; I miss the moon and the lasagna container; I miss taking my shoes on and off; I miss the ablative case." Blank took a breath and sobbed; "I miss getting a mosquito in my eye; I miss hunger; I miss hunger very much; I miss my wife and snow," he said, removed his hands from his face and held himself firmly with his upper arms. "I miss the nondescript potted plants in my office; I miss thunderstorms; the odor of mimeograph stencils; I miss my students, all those who took the qualification in Latin only because it was necessary for the exam; I even miss the fact that I was not able to make Latin interesting for them; I miss the sound of a key in an apartment door; I miss having to check again to see if the stove is still on, because she always, always, always left the stove on." Blank ran his hand over his eyes. "My wife, I mean; of course, not always, but far too often, left the stove on, I mean; I really miss standing at the living room window at night with my hands clasped behind my back; I miss filling out deposit slips; I miss a feeling of fullness and music; I even miss quite unbearable film music; I miss the need to put on a clean shirt, and the feeling of wearing a fresh shirt; the fear of having to die someday; the pharmacist's incredibly ugly sweater; I miss chicken fricassee and PIN numbers; the wind; the range of products on sale in gas stations, that really touching composition of products on sale in service stations, and also," Blank took his hands away from his face; filaments stretched between his fingers. "Pardon me," he said, wiping his hands on his legs, "and besides, I miss you and your strange life, and I miss what I have never known; I miss your wedding; I miss your husband, your husband I miss; I also miss your unpleasant boss and I miss what remains for you, the glued flamingo and the fireman and the peculiar callous remover." Blank ran a hand through his hair, again and again, as if someone had given him a haircut which he wanted nothing to do with.

"And you," I said.

"I miss me too," Blank said. "I miss me, and I miss you; you know you are close to my heart," he stroked the scar on his chest. "You really are close to my heart."

I locked myself in Blank's arms and held him, the way Jacob had held me in his tent, shortly before his phone indicated that there was a new message and the disappearance had long since begun.

"But you are still here, Blank," I said. "You are really here."

Blank smiled at me, the way you smile at a child who claims that all the animals can talk on Christmas day.

"You are close to my heart," I said to Blank's wrinkled, wet neck. "You are closer to my heart than anyone else." Blank stroked my face, my eyes, my nose and mouth, as if he wanted to spread something evenly over it, and then Armin came running up. He let out McQuincey's battle cry, and sprang on my back from behind; and we all fell on and around McQuincey, who was still completely absorbed in thoroughly drying the spaces between his toes.

Blank was asleep; he lay down immediately after we returned from the beach. Armin and I were standing in front of his bed; I stroked Blank's hair; it was full of sand. McQuincey had gone to his room. "Your girlfriend is a very peculiar person," he had said previously to Armin, and meant me. Armin had looked at me quizzically, and I said: "He thinks I'm adorable."

"Are you tired?" Armin now asked. It was two o'clock in the morning, and I was not in the least bit tired. "Then let's go watch a McQuincey film; I've got everything with me," Armin said and went to the door.

I was standing beside Blank's bed. "Come on," Armin said and beckoned me towards him with a sweeping gesture and impatiently, as if I was a child who did not want to leave the playground. "Come on, keep up."

We walked down the hall to his room. It looked exactly like Blank's room and mine; the only difference was a picture of a leaping dolphin with some contemplative saying that hung over his bed. Under the bed a little piece of a picture frame stuck out. Armin kicked the frame under the bed.

I pushed Armin to the side; I knelt down and pulled a gold-framed, medium-sized painting out from under Armin's bed. It showed a rooster on a lush wooded hill. A gold plaque was attached to the bottom of the frame, which said: *The Punctual Rooster*. I lay down on the floor and pulled out everything that was under Armin's bed: a rolled-up rug, a vase and a folded tea trolley.

Armin was sitting on a chair, watching me. I stood up.

"Where is all that from?"

"From a bungalow," Armin said.

"When were you there?"

Armin rolled his eyes. "Today. Just before you came back."

"I thought you were sitting in front of McQuincey's door all the time."

"I was nervous because I thought maybe everything had gone wrong and he wasn't here. To reduce stress, you understand?"

"You steal to reduce stress?"

"Yes," said Armin. "But only sometimes. And only in very

exceptional situations."

I stood in front of him. "It's always worked well," Armin said. "Nothing ever happens. And, my God, nobody misses that stuff; everything is worthless."

"You're really stupid," I said. I had never said that to anyone before. "You need to get help right away."

Armin stood up. "If there's anybody here who needs to get help, it's you," he said. "You, with your perpetual misgivings and objections. You know what—you really need to have sex, as uptight as you are, but I know," he waved his hands around in the air like someone with arachnophobia standing in front of a spider terrarium, "sex is the Holiest of Holies, which you can only have with someone you'll be with forever, even if they fuck other people and then die on you."

I reached out and slapped Armin's face with my open hand. I had never slapped anyone anywhere; I thought about McQuincey and how surprised he had been over his unexpectedly high karate jump, and I struck again. Armin caught my hand and kissed me; I thought, maybe this was also from a karate movie, to catch someone's hand and then kiss them; we stumbled to the closet, Armin pressed himself against me and I kissed him back, because not only did I find my slap exciting, but also because of the way Armin kissed me.

There was a knock on the door. "Somebody's knocking," I said. Armin smiled at me. "I should hope so," he said. Someone knocked again, louder. I pushed Armin away from me, stepped over the tea trolley and went to the door. McQuincey was standing outside. His eyes were glassy. "You want to go swimming again?" he asked. I said that unfortunately, swimming wouldn't work, because Armin and I were about to take an outing to the bungalows. Armin, who had understood the words "Armin," and "bungalows," dropped into his chair with a groan. McQuincey asked if he could accompany us; he didn't have anything else to do; he was not sleeping well, the karate training had been so exhilarating.

I sat at the edge of Blank's bed and stroked his arm. Blank, who usually always woke up immediately, now needed a long time to open his eyes.

"Sorry," I said. "It's true. Armin broke into one of those holiday bungalows this evening."

"Into a vacant bungalow," said Armin, who was standing in the doorway with McQuincey.

I continued to stroke Blank's arm. "We should take the things back before anyone notices anything."

Blank sat up and rubbed his eyebrows, nudging his glasses, which had slipped while he slept to the right and to the left. "He broke in?"

"Yes," I said. "To reduce stress," and threw Armin a look filled with as much contempt as I could manage.

"Yes, to reduce stress," Armin said and struck the door frame. "So what? Other people do yoga."

Blank adjusted his glasses. "Please give me some paper and a pen," Blank said. Blank wanted to draw a detailed map of the bungalow and the road there. "But the road is just straight," Armin said, "and I know exactly what the bungalow looks like inside."

"Still," said Blank, "maps are reassuring."

When we started, it was half past three. There was no longer anyone on the road; Blank said that we should not be lulled into a false sense of security, because of the Dutch window, which was large and had no curtains.

Everyone except McQuincey walked quickly, with our heads lowered. Armin carried his travel bag with the vase, the rolled-up carpet and the painting, McQuincey carried the tea trolley, which I had wrapped in Armin's sheets, Blank held the reassuring map in his hands as if it was the real loot. Since McQuincey was drunk, he unwrapped the tea trolley halfway there, flipped it open and used it as a crutch. The wheels were noisy in the silence; I said that the tea trolley was much too loud, and McQuincey closed it up again elaborately and with a sigh, and relied on me instead, because I happened to be next to him. Blank stopped, consulted his map and then pointed forward. "Straight ahead."

"You don't say," Armin said.

Because I happened to be walking beside him, McQuincey talked to me. He told me about his life, and because he was drunk, he recounted it the same way Armin recounted karate movies. I said repeatedly that it might be better if he told me about his life in the morning, because you can't share in the excitement of life stories on the way to a burglary, but McQuincey would not stop talking. He said that, because things in America weren't going so well, he intended to build a new life in Zandvoort; he had settled on Zandvoort because his late mother was originally from Zandvoort, and had always raved about it. Zandvoort, he said, had been his mother's lost paradise, and I said that he desperately needed to talk a little quieter. McQuincey now whispered very loudly that he was indeed lacking the start-up capital necessary for a new life, because lately in America things weren't going so well, and that he hoped, however, to find a new life in Zandvoort that did not require much start-up capital, the life of a lifeguard, for example, because you probably only needed an affordable swimsuit and a certificate, which should not be a problem, McQuincey said, because, as I had already seen, water was his element.

"What is he saying?" Armin now asked, yet the entire time he had explicitly not asked, because he was explicitly acting bored, as if it were the most boring thing in the world to break in, in order to return stolen property.

"That he's preparing himself for a new career," I explained, and Blank said, "that must be it."

He pointed to one of six identical bungalows, which stood,

staggered, side by side, surrounded by small hedges that were cut so accurately you believed someone had done this work, not with garden shears, but with a dental instrument. The bungalow Armin had broken into seemed to be truly uninhabited; it looked hollow-eyed, but in front of the neighboring bungalows there were cars, and in the neighboring bungalow on the right a faint light burned from the upper floor.

The idea to bring the stuff back to the bungalow had been a good idea, but the dark bungalow which we were now standing in front of was much more concrete than a good idea. Breaking into the bungalow was not a good idea, and I suddenly thought that returning worthless stuff was not worth the risk and that in the long run Armin had always done well with burglaries instead of yoga, and possibly, I thought, we would not do well with a return burglary and instead get caught and taken into custody and get into a hell of a mess. I thought of Evelyn, who had always encouraged me to get angry at Jacob, and had therefore made me take an aggression test, an aggression test that Evelyn's psychiatrist had published in his book. The test revealed that my level of aggression was at minus eight, and break-ins are not expected from someone with a potential for aggression of minus eight.

"The whole thing is a little tricky," I said. "We're going to be in hell of a mess."

"It's not tricky at all," Armin said. "It's so easy that it's boring, and we are not going to be in hell of a mess, but inside the damned bungalow." He said this as if a hell of a mess was a more desirable place, as if instead of a hell of a mess it was just a big party, which he had missed because he was being forced to stand around with us in a non-smoking disco.

"Blank, what do you think?" I asked, because Blank, after all, had a reassuring map. Blank looked at the gravel road that led to the bungalow. It was a gravel road that, as soon as we stepped on it, would begin to make a lot of noise. Blank raised his arms and looked at me skeptically. "Blank thinks that we're good to go," I said; I said it above all to reassure myself. 'He believes the risk is negligible."

"You misunderstood me," Blank said, and Armin said. "That's what I've been saying."

We walked across the noisy gravel path and around the bungalow. A window on the back side was tilted open. "This is so ridiculously simple," Armin said, took two wire coat hangers from his pocket and used them to construct something that looked like a poor excuse for a fishing rod. Armin wound the coat hanger tool through the opening in the window, pulled up the window handle and opened the window. "Here you go," he said. "You don't even have to climb very high."

Armin swung over the windowsill. McQuincey sat down clumsily on the grass and said he would keep watch. McQuincey did not look like a reliable guard, but because Armin looked like someone with an aggressive potential of plus nine to me I did not say that, and instead said that, in that case, Blank and I would also come in.

"Do that," Armin said.

"I can stay here and help Mr. McQuincey, if you prefer," Blank said. "During a break-in, keeping a diligent look-out is essential." I nodded. Blank handed me his map as if it was a last will and testament. I climbed through the window and found myself in the living room. The nearly full moon provided a dim light, and it had a stale lemon scent. Above a mustard-colored, three-piece suite of furniture hung several paintings; Armin's *Punctual Rooster* was part of a series. *The Proud Deer* was hanging there, *The Powerful Wild Boar* and *The Watchful Fox*, all of them standing on the same wooded hill. I thought of Armin's grandfather and the pig, and wondered why Armin hadn't opted for the powerful boar, because his grandfather would have certainly been pleased by that. I decided to ask Armin about that later, because you don't talk about gift ideas in the middle of a burglary.

Armin was sitting on a mustard-colored chair; he looked annoyed, as if he was thinking about all that he had missed out on in a hell of a mess. I opened the bag, took out the *Punctual Rooster*, took off my shoes, climbed on the sofa and hung the painting on the free nail. "Is that good?" I asked.

"That's good."

I turned around. Armin had his eyes closed and was rubbing his temples with his thumb and middle finger.

"You didn't even look."

Armin sighed and looked apathetically at the rooster, and then at me. "A little bit more to the left."

I shifted the picture, and then I got off the sofa and looked at the rooster. "Perfect," I said. "And the tea trolley, where does that belong?"

Armin gestured lackadaisically toward the sideboard next to the TV.

"Beside that," he said. I unwrapped the tea trolley, opened it and placed it next to the sideboard.

"Like this?"

"Yes." Armin yawned. I placed the tea trolley at a slight angle, because I thought that gave the tea trolley a somewhat whimsical look and made it look a little less lost beside the massive sideboard. The vase belonged on the sideboard; there was already a rubber mat to place it on. I regretted that we had not thought of flowers. "And the rug?"

Armin pointed to the floor in front of his chair. I spread out the rug and straightened the tassels. "You know, Armin, that's how it is," I said while I worked. "We are simply giving back everything that doesn't belong to us. When you have something that really doesn't belong to you, and I don't necessarily mean just stolen things, but also those things that you once believed belonged to you, that you actually have a claim to, just because they came along with you for a while, then at some point you have to give them back again; that's how it is, plain and simple. You return them to the place where they belong, for which they are intended, and which someone else has chosen. That's the best thing for everybody involved. What do you think? Is it okay?" I asked, gesturing at the carpet.

Armin nodded.

"Or perhaps you prefer a diagonal?"

Armin nodded.

"We can do that," I said and lay the rug at a diagonal and then straight again. "We could also deliberately and voluntarily leave something here that belongs to us. I mean, which we *believe* belongs to us. Then it is no longer with us, plain and simple, but somewhere else, but it's still there, even if we never see it again."

"A great idea," Armin said and yawned. "The best thing would be our passports."

The carpet now lay in the way that suited it best, the tea trolley was in the position that fit it most, the *Punctual Rooster* looked colorful in spite of the gloom and the vase seemed to blossom.

I looked at the clock that hung beside the animal prints. It was three twenty. Putting everything back had gone quickly.

I looked around the living room. "That went well," I said, and suddenly thought that I knew how Armin had felt after he had climbed down from my kitchen window sill, after being in the rain gutter searching for a fire that did not exist.

Armin smiled wearily. "I still have something," he said, bent over his bag and pulled out a heavy gold ashtray shaped like a hand, and pointed to the coffee table beside the sofa.

"Thanks," I said and arranged the ashtray on the coffee table, first at an angle, then straight. When I turned to Armin, he was asleep. I stroked his head. Armin blinked and held out his hand; I pulled him out of the chair and behind me to the window.

"Wait a minute," I said. Armin sat on the windowsill.

I looked at Blank's map and went to the bathroom, reached into my pocket and put Jacob's *Tears Again* in the mirrored cabinet over the sink.

"Are we finished now?" Armin asked when I returned. I nodded, and we climbed out the window. Outside, McQuincey and Blank were sleeping; Blank's head lay on McQuincey's shoulder, McQuincey's snore was louder than any gravel road could ever be. I shook McQuincey's shoulder and said we could go now, everything was back in its place.

McQuincey rubbed his eyes. "It was ridiculously easy," Armin said. Blank looked at me and said, "You got a tan."

We stayed for two days and three nights. Armin spent his days with McQuincey. They watched McQuincey's movies and during it Armin told him what scenes and climatic moments he found particularly successful, and McQuincey did not understand a word, but he understood Armin's enthusiasm perfectly. They went swimming; on the beach McQuincey taught Armin karate, although he had never learned it, and fortunately McQuincey's karate needed no explanation. On the next to the last day they both got the same anchor needled on the same spot on the left upper arm. Armin got the idea, and McQuincey thought that it was the appropriate tattoo for an aspiring lifeguard. I asked Armin if the needles were painful; Armin shrugged his shoulders and said it was about as painful as if someone was holding a just blown out match to your arm.

I spent both days with Blank; we walked along the sea, sipping drinks in the beach pavilions that were sweet and thick, and we went cycling. I rented a tandem. We rode long and straight. On our left was the sea, lying on our right was the dunes where high grass swayed, like the photos in the hallway of the pension. Blank sat in the back. The tandem was a bit too small for him; when he pedaled his sharp knees rose almost to his chest. His black hair and his black coat tails fluttered in the wind. I often turned around to him; it was fun to see Blank looking happy. "Look forwards," he would cry then, because we threatened to tip over every time I turned around to him. Otherwise we said nothing, and we were silent and looked at the landscape; a light warm drizzle fell, which you could direct your face up into.

"We could sing something," I said. We sang *Sailor, Your Home is the Sea*, because Blank had often sung it to me, before we had first bought the astronaut food, and because there was no other song that we both knew. Blank then sang *Boy, Come Back Soon*, and I hummed along. Then I sang the title song from *Karate Kid II*, the song about the glory of love. I didn't remember much of it, but what I still remembered I sang very loudly and Blank hummed along.

The three nights I spent with Armin. When Blank fell asleep and I was still awake, I walked down the hallway making intermittent contact with reality and knocked on Armin's door. "There you are," Armin would say, and when I came in he lay in his bed, naked and on his back, with his arms folded behind his head, under the contemplative dolphin. After Jacob's disappearance, I had not expected that my body would be used for anything else besides walking or sitting or sleeping, that it would have to deal with anything else, like shower gel, or ailments, or weather; I had, when it came to my body, not reckoned with the absurd, and even less with the fact that it would have to deal with Armin, of all people.

When Armin and I lay in his single bed together for the first time, I could not stop thinking about Jacob, how it had been, when Jacob's disappearance had already begun, to sleep with Jacob. Sex with Jacob, at the time of his disappearance, was like an event held by an acquaintance that only a few people attend; no one, in fact, except friends and acquaintances, who are trying during and after the event to be particularly enthusiastic, to conceal the absence of others, which you cannot or can only very briefly conceal, and later, when the acquaintance thinks back on his event, he no longer thinks about the friends and acquaintances who stressed their enthusiasm, he thinks only that there was nobody there.

The first time in Armin's single bed, I thought, as Armin and I kissed, not just about Jacob and Alina, but also about Jacob and Alina in Jacob's and my bed. I could not imagine Jacob and Alina in bed, so I imagined the worst, and the worst in this case was the very best, and finally Armin stopped kissing me, and said, "I am kissing you right now, and I'm doing it pretty well, so it would be nice if you would stop thinking about any shit."

When I slept with Armin for the first time and fell out of his single bed twice and Armin once, Armin said the same things he also said about karate movies; he pointed out particular highlights to me and prepared me for the crucial scenes. "Watch, you'll like this," he would say, or: "this spot is especially good," or: "That's unbelievable, right? The best is yet to come." Armin would say that until I would say, "Now shut up." I had never said that to anyone, and Armin would stop talking and instead lapse into sign language. Armin's body was large and heavy, and my body was fortunately somewhat larger and heavier than I had remembered it. The first time I noticed I no longer completely remembered Jacob's body, probably because it was an event at the end, which nobody actually attended. It was also an event with Armin, but where nothing had to be stressed, because everyone was there, even the ones you did not expect, and even those you did not know personally. After we had slept together for the first time, Armin signed after a while, while we were silent and I looked down at my body, with one hand on his tightly pressed lips and the other painting question marks in the air, which stood for the question of whether he would be allowed to say anything again.

"You're welcome to," I said.

Armin leaned over me and smiled. "*Hard and soft, tension and relaxation,*" he said in a tone that sounded like he was giving me the recipe for a cake we had just eaten. "*All in combination with the proper breathing.*"

I pushed Armin away from me a little and looked at him.

"Tantra?" I asked, startled. "Karate rule number 19," Armin said.

After part of the night I spent with Armin, I went back into Blank's and my room. I always hoped that Blank would be asleep, and every time I combed my hair with Armin's brush before I went back to our room, and, because the only thing I found in Armin's toiletry bag besides Axe Shock musk oil, which I wanted to cover up, was sore throat spray, I sprayed myself behind the ears and wrists with a little sore throat spray. On the first two nights Blank was actually asleep, but the third he was in bed, wide awake.

"Hello," I said, thinking about my parents, the night I had encountered them in the hallway after I lost my virginity. Because I was afraid that you could see in my face that I had lost my virginity, I had hoped fervently that they would be sleeping, but they were both standing there, in knotted bathrobes, side by side, staring at me. My parents were against me losing my virginity; they were mainly against me losing my virginity at fifteen, and they were especially against me losing my virginity to someone who smoked and drove his father's Porsche. My mother stared at the middle of my face with particular intensity, and then she turned away and broke out in tears, as if she had just learned that I only had a few months left to live.

I walked past Blank's bed to mine, lay down and pulled the blanket up under my chin. I was afraid that Blank would first stare at me intensely and then burst into tears, but I feared more that he would do what the parents of my girlfriends at school had done after they lost their virginity—namely, smiled and asked if it had been good. I pretended I was asleep at once, and after a While Blank said: "Axe Shock Eucalyptus."

I pretended hard that I had fallen asleep on the spot. "You are really hoping that I won't say anything," Blank said.

"True," I said. "I would like that very much."

Again we were silent for a while, until Blank said, "but unfortunately that won't work," as he rose from his bed. He came over to me and stood beside my bed and looked at me as if I had just received an award, a prize for a breakthrough invention, a milestone for the research, and as if he also wanted to congratulate me.

"This is excellent," he said. "I must say, I think this is excellent."

I turned on my side. "Please, Blank, can we go to sleep now?"

Blank went back to bed. I could tell that he was not sleeping, and he finally turned on the bedside lamp. I sat up. Blank sat in bed with a newspaper and looked at me gleefully. "I can't sleep," he said cheerfully. I let my head fall back on the pillow. "I can," I said.

The next morning we packed our things, carried them to the car and then had breakfast one last time in the guest house. Piano music by Richard Clayderman played from a small speaker on the ceiling. Blank did not eat because he did not have to eat anything, Armin ate nothing, because he had a lump in his throat, which had nothing to do with Richard Clayderman, but a lot with McQuincey, and McQuincey ate nothing, because he had a hangover. I drizzled chocolate sprinkles over my second piece of toast. "You can all see each other again," I said. "Holland isn't in some other galaxy." Armin nodded and poked at his butter. He looked like someone who has just had a blown out match held to his bare arm.

"Good luck with your new life," I said to McQuincey as we stood outside the car. McQuincey shook my hand and wished me the same. Then he held out his outstretched hand in the direction where he believed Blank was standing; Blank moved to the spot quickly and grabbed McQuincey's hand.

Then Armin and McQuincey embraced; they embraced silently and slapped each other on the shoulders, like friends in a film who have gone through many adventures together and now have to say goodbye, and don't need to waste a lot of words. Nevertheless, Armin's and McQuincey's hugging and slapping and silence lasted much longer than it did in such a movie, and when they drew apart, Armin said hoarsely: "In Okinawa, honor have no time limit." I tried to translate it. Tears welled up in McQuincey's eyes. "Karate Kid" he said, and you couldn't tell whether he was referring to the source or using it as a nickname.

We got into the car. I sat behind the wheel, Armin got in the back, and Blank sat in the passenger's seat, and, because he was much bigger than Armin, he jerked the seat back. We drove off and waved. Armin knelt on the back seat and waved through the rear window, where there was still just a bit of the word *Married* and the word *Just* was still easy to recognize.

I watched as McQuincey gradually grew smaller in the rearview mirror. He waved with evenly swinging arms; his elaborate, quiet waving seemed to have almost nothing to do with us, as if he was waving just to wave, and finally McQuincey, who had grown much smaller, looked as if an existence as a professional waver was the new life he had envisioned without start-up capital.

Your Favorite Song

I unlocked the front door. Blank and I walked through the hallway and I asked him if he also found that the floorboards creak differently when they are no longer used. Blank paused, rocked on a board and nodded.

We had been gone almost a week. Nevertheless, I had expected that the house plant would have dried up and there would be thick dust lying on the floor, that huge cobwebs would be stretched across the room and someone would have covered the furniture with white sheets. We walked over the floorboards, which needed to tune themselves, into the kitchen, the bedroom, the living room. Nothing was covered, it had already been dusty, and the houseplant was a palm tree.

Next to the palm was the flamingo. When it had broken, it had waited for the time when Jacob and I no longer encouraged it and no longer watched it; it had postponed its destruction until Jacob had vanished and I had also vanished, at least as much as you can vanish when you're still there; therefore it would not have surprised me if the flamingo had used my absence for yet another break, but it was unharmed.

In the living room I looked at the answering machine. Every time Jacob and I had come home after being away for a long time, Jacob found it astonishing to think that the answering machine had probably been flashing the entire time we were gone, because someone might have left a message shortly after we had closed the door behind us. "Just imagine how exhausting that must be," Jacob had said, "to blink for three weeks, for absolutely nothing." Then he liberated the answering machine and pressed *Play*.

I looked at the blinking answering machine, and for a moment I thought that maybe it would be Jacob, that as soon as I pressed *Play*, he would say that everything had been a misunderstanding, a colossal, egregious, global misunderstanding, and that in reality nothing of importance had happened, only things that in my absence had proved to be meaningless, like Alina, for example; like, for example, the accident; that luckily both Alina and the accident didn't turn out the way that he had imagined it; that he was sorry he had inconvenienced me and he hoped that I had rested well during my vacation. I thought for a moment that if I pressed *Play*, Jacob would say that he would call again tonight, and say: "See you later."

I pressed *Play*. My mother said: "We haven't talked to each other in a long time," and that I really should call her. The telephone company said that they had an attractive offer for me. The one before that and the next to last message were from Bengt; he had left it on the answering machine only today. Bengt said it was all a misunderstanding and that things with the new English translator had not worked out as he had imagined, ultimately, he said, our profession depends on creativity, to be sure, but above all on accuracy, and that he hoped I had rested well during my vacation, that he would call again tonight and now wanted to inquire tentatively whether I could translate an instruction manual by tomorrow. I crossed my arms.

The last message was from Armin, who we had dropped off at a subway station earlier. He said: "I'm bringing pizza," although we were not certain that Armin was still coming.

Blank rocked back and forth on a floorboard. "That's an attractive offer," he said.

"Bengt or the pizza?"

"Bengt, I mean," Blank said, smiling. "But also the pizza, of course."

Then he ran his fingers through his hair, and that was when I saw the hole.

Blank paused, his hand still on his head, and looked at me with fear. "You're quite pale," he said. "What is it?"

I pointed to Blank's arm and walked over to him.

The hole was in the inner surface of his upper arm, a few inches above his armpit. It was a walnut-sized hole you could see through; you could see through the hole in Blank's arm as if through a tiny window.

I suddenly turned very red, as if I had forgotten something important. "What's that?" I whispered. Blank looked at me.

"What?" He asked.

"There's a hole in your arm," I whispered, and now Blank was pale.

"Don't you see it?" I asked. Blank shook his head.

"Does it hurt?"

He shook his head again.

"What does that mean?" I asked, still whispering, as if Blank and I had created a breakthrough invention which no one must learn about, because if it fell into the wrong hands it would have devastating consequences.

"I don't know," Blank whispered, "I have no idea what that means," and I could see that Blank had lied to me for the first time, that he very well had an idea what it meant.

I went into the bathroom, opened the cabinet above the mirror which no longer contained Jacob's expensive toothpaste or his deodorant, so there was space in it for the Band-Aids I had bought at the pharmacy in order to buy time for the question about astronaut food. I took two Band-Aids out of the box, wondering whether Band-Aids also adhered to suit sleeves, and went back into the living room. Blank raised his arm; I stuck two Band-Aids over the hole, one in front and one in the rear. Blank knocked on the Band-Aid and twisted his arm back and forth. "It's sticking," he said.

"You really don't see it?" I asked.

"No," said Blank, "the Band-Aid—I see that. But I did not see the hole."

The Band-Aid stuck, and we did not mention it again.

I made an appointment with the ophthalmologist. Some time ago, during a follow-up, he had determined that everything was fine. As I sat on his chair, I said: "I can't see some things properly."

The ophthalmologist raised his eyebrows. "What kind of things?" he asked. "Especially small ones? Or especially far away?"

"Things close up," I said, and I turned red because I did not know how to convince the eye doctor that I could not see something properly which, according to experience, no one else could see at all; how I could explain it to him without having him transfer me to someone who would ask constructive questions and had a sealed cupboard full of pills that made you light and tired.

The ophthalmologist shined a light in my eyes and conducted an eye test. Then he said: "Everything is perfectly fine."

"Are you quite sure?" I asked, as if perfectly fine was a devastating diagnosis.

"No doubt," said the ophthalmologist.

"Thanks anyway," I said.

Monday to Friday, I went to translate. Evelyn was back again. You could tell by looking at her that she hadn't had any marzipan. And the psychiatrist had returned. I imagined him sitting on the still unpacked suitcases in his office and trying to reach the patients; I imagined that the patients on the telephone pretended they were not at home, because in the meantime they had found someone to whom they could confide their secrets and who could pretend at any time that they are not at home. Evelyn translated next to me at her desk, which was loaded with photos. Because I thought my desk looked bare and I had never actually thought having framed photos of loved ones was a bad habit, I arranged a few. I put out a photo of Jacob, where he looked happy and a little blurry. He had taken it with a self-timer and sent it to me when he had been in America, while I counted the days and had experienced only the bare minimum. I put out a photo of Blank, Armin and McQuincey, standing in front of a Caribbean beach at sunset. The beach was a big contemplative photograph in the hallway of the guest house. The picture filled the entire background; it was a glossy photo and reflected a little, so you could see the flash of my camera on the Caribbean Sea. McQuincey and Armin stood side by side, laughing into the camera and had their arms placed around each other's shoulders. Blank was standing beside Armin, smiling and pointing his index finger at Armin's chest. Armin's shirt was wide open; you could see a part of the *Nothing* that looked like a corrected *Nofking*. "Nofking is forever," Blank had said when I took the photo. "I'd like to meet this Nofking sometime."

"Who is this illustrious pair?" Evelyn said.

"He's Armin," I said. "The fireman. And that's Ralph McQuincey."

Evelyn took the photo in her hand and examined McQuincey extensively. "I've seen him on TV," she said then.

"Really?" I asked, and looked at Evelyn in amazement. "Yes," she said and looked at me in amazement too. "Didn't you say he was a movie star?"

"Yes."

"And what is so amazing about somebody seeing a movie star on television?"

I looked at the photo. "Nothing, of course," I said.

When I came home at night, Blank was there and had cooked and read and would be standing at the window. Every second evening Armin came by. I opened the door, Armin walked silently into the kitchen and sat down, talked about overturned trucks and false alarms, and, after he had asked in vain on several evenings whether or not I had a little of the astronauts' food in the house, he began to bring it himself.

At night Armin came with me into my bed, which had once been Jacob's bed and mine. Blank slept on the sofa. "It's time for you to go back to your bed," he had said. When I had first gotten back into the bed, Armin got in with me, and that made it less upsetting, just as I had thought. The first night with Armin in Jacob's bed and mine was awkward because, as we lay in bed, I thought that the bed desperately needed to go somewhere else, and so we got up again and moved the wardrobe and the bed; we moved it a total of one and a half times across the room, until it was finally in a position that Jacob never ever would have wanted.

After that, Armin fell exhausted onto the bed and rubbed his shoulder, which had grown tight from repeated lifting of the bed. I plopped down beside him. "Armin," I said, "it's really good that you're here." That was true. It was true, and that there was basically nothing connecting me to Armin was also true, but that didn't matter; nobody had to say that, because saying it was about as unnecessary as telling an aunt that you don't like her porcelain flamingo.

Armin smiled. "I know," he said, clasped his hands behind his head and sighed contentedly. "I'm pretty much all that you need." I thought that for Armin, that was a relatively modest sentence. "Pretty much everything?" I asked. "Then what do I still need, in your opinion?"

Armin sat up and looked at me in astonishment. "Blank, of course," he said.

I expected again and again to meet Alina on the street and one morning I expected it particularly strongly.

"Something absurd is going to happen today," I had said to Blank at breakfast. "I'm sure of it."

"What?" Blank asked. "That hasn't been revealed yet," I said, and

Blank smiled and responded that he was very curious about it. Blank and I did not meet Alina, but something else absurd happened. It happened at the weekly market. We had purchased potatoes and pears. Blank was telling me something about a subtlety in a translation from the Latin, and I would have listened to him gladly but I could not, because I suddenly felt sick and I was getting worse. When I stopped Blank broke off, looked at me and said, "You are quite green."

"I suddenly feel very funny," I said. I took several deep breaths, which did not help; I had a suspicion about what was about to happen, namely something unpleasant and something that breathing could not help, and then I rested an arm on Blank's shoulder and I vomited right next to his shoes and right next to a box of broccoli, which a sales lady grabbed in horror.

"Sorry," I said and wiped my mouth. Blank and a customer in the vegetable aisle looked at me anxiously. The customer managed to find me a folding stool. I sat down and rested my head on my hands.

"I don't know, I probably ate something bad," I said to Blank, and I noticed that Blank noticed that I had just lied to him for the first time, because I had really had a hunch for awhile, a hunch I was avoiding the way I had recently been avoiding unpaid bills, namely in the hope that they would eventually, politely stop coming. I also had a hunch that in thinking about odd things I had not been thorough or creative enough, because I had not thought of the oddest, the oddest of all, and besides, I had a hunch that sometimes you have a hunch about when things start, though not their extent or their impact.

The gynecologist was a humorous doctor. In her waiting room there hung a clock with a mirror-image clock face. In the frame of the clock engraved text said: *Sometimes everything just runs in reverse.*

Blank and I watched in silence, as ten minutes ran backwards. Then I went into the treatment room.

"That can happen," the doctor said as I took a seat in the treatment chair and after she had explained that contraceptive coils inserted into the body were in most cases, but not always, adequate prevention. "It's extremely rare. It happens in approximately four out of a hundred women. It happened to you."

I imagined the contraceptive coil in my body as an instrument with an inadequate signaling unit; that perhaps, when it had noticed its incompetency, had flashed in my body like an exhausted answering machine in an abandoned apartment.

The doctor pointed to the monitor and to something that looked like a comma.

"It's pulsing already," she said and smiled.

When I came back to the waiting room, Blank got up and hastened to meet me. He had thumbed through a magazine and still held it in his hand; it was the magazine *Parents*—on the cover a young family laughed in the snow.

"It's pulsing already," I said.

Back at home, I sat on the kitchen floor because I was dizzy. I sat on the exact spot where I had been sitting after Jacob's funeral and had found that life would no longer be possible, where Blank had discovered the callous remover and said that all major decisions are made on the basis of incomplete data, and had asked if I could be one hundred percent sure that life was no longer possible, and I started to protest, and those protestations had been signs of life. I sat on the exact spot; everything was swimming and I thought about getting on with my life, and about the signs of life, and then I thought, "Get up right now, and don't on any account just continue to sit here," but that didn't work, because my legs felt like they were filled with air. Blank sat down beside me. I looked at him, and he looked at his shoes.

"It won't work," I said.

Blank grabbed my hand and stroked my palm.

"What exactly won't work?" he asked softly, "having it or not having it?"

Both, I thought and said, "The first one."

Blank nodded. He nodded at length, and then the doorbell rang.

"That's Armin," I said. Blank continued to nod. I did not open the door, and imagined Armin in his fireman's uniform, how he looked through the peephole, somewhat distorted, how he rang again, waited and then walked away. It rang once again and then no more.

I felt my legs. "Will you come walk with me?" I asked. Blank continued to nod.

Nearby there was an artificial lake, reached by a gravel road. Blank and I walked around the lake again and again, all night long, and because the lake was quite small, it made you dizzy. I walked quickly. Blank walked a few steps behind me; he also walked quickly, and sometimes when I stopped abruptly, Blank ran into me. I explained to Blank why the first choice would not work. I explained it at length, and whenever I said something decisive I turned to Blank and then he nodded like someone who has just heard the explanation for a ground-breaking formula and had not understood a word of it, but nods anyway, because the one who has explained the formula is supposed to be an authority. Jacob and I had tried for a long time to have a child. We had, when Jacob's disappearance began, given up. I was relieved that it had not worked, not only because Jacob disappeared, but also because I was sure that my body was a rather inhospitable terrain for a child, that nothing would come out intact. I did not know how I knew that—no one had told me—but I knew it, as if everyone had said it; it was much like the fact that you cannot make a Greyhound out of a Saint Bernard. Although, I said to Blank, perhaps that was no longer true, because by now, due to groundbreaking inventions, you could make any dog from any other dog, but that doesn't count and did not change the nature of the dog because it continued to have the character of a Saint Bernard.

I stopped; Blank ran into me, and we stumbled.

I turned to Blank. "It's not easy," I said.

I thought about everything that you needed for a child; you needed an appropriate body and the proper frame of mind, a decent life and a role model and money, and inner strength and serenity; for a child you needed to find inner peace and at the same time be able to venture outside yourself and perform other feats.

"Shall we go home?" Blank asked.

"No," I said, and then I told him what I would say to the counselor from Planned Parenthood, namely that the facts spoke for themselves. "My husband died recently," I said to Blank for the sake of practice, "after he had already disappeared, and now I'm pregnant by a hooligan, small-time criminal fireman, whom I barely know, and the pregnancy is taking place in a rather inhospitable terrain for a child, because until recently my body was sustained with nothing but astronaut food."

"With a high-calorie, vitamin-rich nutritional liquid supplement," Blank said.

"With a high-calorie nutritional liquid supplement. And the worst thing," I said. "is that the one, the one who has stood beside me and sustained me with the high-calorie nutritional liquid supplement, has recently developed a hole, a hole in his upper arm, and we don't talk about it. He knows what it means and I don't; only that it's something devastating."

I told the counselor from Planned Parenthood almost exactly the same thing. She nodded with understanding, reached for the required form and sat down, but before she signed it, she suddenly started to ask constructive questions. I did not want any constructive questions because they would not be constructive, but have a corrosive effect. I knew that with constructive questions in my head I would be able to sleep even less than I already was, because of the pulsations. Because questions shouldn't be coming up at the same frequency, I said to the counselor: "I'm a Saint Bernard," and then, without any additional questions, she filled out the required form.

The next night I went to Blank, who was sleeping in the living room, and woke him. When I was lying in bed, I imagined I could hear how it was beating through the abdominal wall. "It's beating," I said, "I hear it beating all the time. Is that normal?"

Blank sat up and adjusted his glasses. "May I?" he asked, putting his hand first on my belly, and then on my chest. "That is your heart," he said. I looked at Blank's hand on my chest; the light was dim. Nevertheless, I saw the hole in Blank's wrist, a raisin-sized hole on his right wrist that you could see through.

I went into the bathroom, got a Band-Aid, cut off a small section and went back into the living room. Blank sat on the sofa and focused on his palms. His hair was disheveled.

I took Blank's hand and bandaged his wrist. It was quick. I held his hand in mine and stroked his palm, as if I wanted to spread something.

Blank's palm was large and surprisingly smooth. The lines were not deep and they stretched like a frantic and therefore not very skillfully spun spider's web over his skin. I looked at his palm for a long time, and suddenly on Blank's palm, as if on a small, slightly rumpled canvas, and the way it's supposed to be when you die, there was a cinematic synopsis running, a brief synopsis of what had happened so far. It ran so fast that you could not identify everything. Caring for the school vegetable garden flashed by. The paintings of images without monsters in ice cream colors and the vision of the dermatologist flashed by and the eternal calming herbal tea in the study, which had tasted awful. All the vacations, which I had told half-truths about, because the whole truth had always been that we stayed in quiet residential compounds, flashed by, Jacob flashed by,

Jacob for the first time and with his sign over the dental chair, the wedding at the lake and the pastor with his unsurpassable love, my bandaged eyes after the surgery, Jacob's body flashed by and Alina's too, the driver who was responsible for the accident flashed by and the coffin, the nutritional liquid supplement, which had tasted awful, flashed by, and Blank, Blank most of all: Blank on my bathtub and Blank at the sea; Blank flashed by in my kitchen and in the guest house; Armin flashed by, the way he sat in my kitchen for the first time and had said: "I can easily imagine the chest of drawers painted light green;" the bungalow flashed by and the clock and in the humorous doctor's waiting room, with the hands that ran the wrong way round flashed by.

Blank, who had first been staring at me and then at his palm, took his hand out of mine and held it very close to his face. "What's that?" he asked. "Yet another hole?"

"No," I said. "Just this one."

Then the doorbell rang. I opened the door; Armin walked past me silently into the kitchen and sat down. I sat beside him at the table.

"I don't mind that I haven't heard from you," Armin said.

"Good," I said, and then I felt sick. "I'm sorry," I said, and then ran into the bathroom. When I returned to the kitchen Blank, who stood in the doorway, held me by the arm.

"You have to tell him," he whispered. I took Blank's hand away from my arm and sat down again at the kitchen table. "Diarrhea?" Armin asked. "Yes," I said.

Armin nodded. "And otherwise?"

Blank came to the table and stood next to Armin. "Armin," he said. "There has been a pregnancy. If I understand correctly, she doesn't want to have the child any more than you do, probably. The appointment is tomorrow at eight thirty. You have to come along. You need to stand by her."

Blank had spoken aloud, and I was turning red, because if it's totally absurd to get pregnant, perhaps Armin could also hear Blank for once.

Armin looked around the kitchen. "Where is Blank?"

"Asleep," I said.

Blank sat down on the empty kitchen chair. He sat down like someone who has just carried extremely heavy boxes and has now learned that all the boxes must unfortunately go somewhere else. He avoided looking at me, and I avoided looking at him.

"Has he gone to see his wife already?" Armin asked.

"No."

Armin nodded, and because I was silent, he said: "I was allowed to help the breathing gear specialist today," and he described in detail the characteristics of various filters. I wondered why Armin was still pretending to be a fireman. I was sure that he was no fireman, something else, but not a fireman; the uniform still looked fake.

"He just doesn't feel up to it," I said after a while.

"Huh?" Armin declared.

"He just doesn't trust himself with his wife," I said, and now Blank and I could no longer avoid looking at each other.

"Why not? The worst is behind him. He's already dead." Armin shaped his hands into a funnel and held it in front of his mouth. "Dr. Blank," he cried, "what is it like when you die?"

Blank winced. Armin had yelled right into Blank's face. "Be quiet," I hissed and waved my arms.

"Listen, regarding Blank and his wife," Armin stretched his legs and took a big swig from the nutritional liquid supplement he had brought along. "Tell him the following: *If you're afraid of the heat, get closer to the fire.*" Armin said it like Blank, when he quoted something in Latin. "*It won't get any hotter.*"

"Karate rule number one thousand," I said.

"Lao Tzu?" Blank asked.

"Ralph McQuincey in *The Iron Fist of Death*," Armin said.

The doctor, whose receptionist looked like the daughter of Jacob's receptionist and who accepted the required form, was named Dr. Joyland; that was actually his name. Evelyn had been to see him twice. She had written down his name and phone number for me and said:

"His name is doesn't indicate anything."

The waiting room was full of suffering patients who sat close together on the folding chairs. Blank was the only man. The walls were bright blue and decorated with fish. A woman with a child explained it by saying that if you get pregnant, it feels like you have a water-filled bag containing a fish in your stomach and that you notice it and it makes you happy when the fish swims against the bag. Blank sat next to me and pretended he was reading a pamphlet about cervical cancer prevention. I also had a brochure in my hand, a brochure about something else, and tried not to touch the woman next to me with my thighs, because she looked like she would break, as if at the slightest touch she would change her shape like a puff of smoke.

Because I was trying hard to keep my thighs away from her, my leg started to shake. I tried to think of the facts which spoke for themselves, meaning Jacob and that he was dead, and my body and that it was inhospitable, and Armin and that I hardly knew him, and Blank and that he had a hole in his arm and a hole in his wrist. The facts spoke not only for themselves, they were downright chatty; they rolled over in the face of factuality. My leg stopped shivering; I leaned back, gently, on account of the malleable woman, and at that moment Blank lowered his brochure and whispered, "This is what I have always wanted to ask you: how is everything really going with your Uncle Arno?"

"What?" I whispered. "What made you think about that now?"

The woman with the thigh that I could not touch looked at me.

"I wanted you to think about something really pleasant," Blank said. "What did Uncle Arno really do for a living? He's retired, right?" I didn't say anything and looked at Blank blankly. "It was worth a try," he said and looked at his brochure again.

I had told Blank about Uncle Arno when I had told him about my wedding. Since then, I hadn't thought any more about Uncle Arno. I seldom thought about Uncle Arno and tried to push him behind the wordy facts, but Uncle Arno, as he was entitled to by Blank's reference and as though he was also a significant fact, elbowed his way to the front again and again, like a child in a school theatrical performance during the final applause, elbowing in front of the lead characters, even though he was only playing someone with a single line or a tree.

Uncle Arno was my father's cousin. My father had told my mother during their first date that Uncle Arno was the handsomest man in his entire large family. Eyes, Uncle Arno had, blue like an enchanted lake, and a figure Uncle Arno had, slim and as tall as a cypress tree. When my mother met my father's parents and siblings that night, as my father announced his engagement with my mother, his parents and siblings raved so excessively about Uncle Arnos' eyes and figure, that my mother thought on the one hand that my father should for goodness' sake not marry her, but uncle Arrno, and on the other hand increasingly figured that she, once she saw him, would no longer want to marry my father, but Uncle Arno.

Uncle Arno was a beauty—everyone said so. Mother met him at a big family celebration. "Where is he then?" my mother asked her future mother-in-law. "There," the mother-in-law said, and pointed, as my mother explained it, to the opposite of Uncle Arno, a very cheerful and boisterous man, who hurried towards my mother and greeted her with a slightly damp kiss on the hand, and whose eyes were not enchanted, but somehow chlorine blue with thick bags underneath, and his figure, if any, was that of a very expansive cypress. He beamed at my mother; my mother stared at him and did not know what to say; in any case she absolutely did not want to say what was on her tongue, but then she said it; she could not help it; it blurted out. "You are not at all so beautiful," my mother whispered.

Uncle Arno smiled. "I know," he whispered. "Shall we still dance?"

My mother and Uncle Arno danced for a long time, because Uncle Arno was a fantastic dancer, so fantastic, that my mother, if only for a moment, wondered whether she really should marry my father.

I heard about Uncle Arno's legendary beauty only after I had known him for a long time already. As a child I loved uncle Arno, because every time we saw each other, he held me upside down in the air; nobody else did that, and when, as a child in elementary school, I witnessed for the first time how my grandmother and my father started to conjure up Uncle Arno's beauty, I asked several times whether they actually meant Uncle Arno, or whether perhaps a second Uncle Arno existed, who was enchanted and tall as a cypress and who had emigrated, and my grandmother and my father looked at me as if they did not understand the question.

I thought, because Uncle Arno, expansive as he was, had now solidly urged himself forward in the face of the much-evoked facts, solely about him and how he had held me upside down in the air. I had no idea what Uncle Arno was doing here. Maybe he would not be driven away because all the claims about him had been false, because he had been the content opposite of all the claims about himself and suddenly I ached like never before, to be the content opposite of all the claims about me. Maybe Uncle Arno would not be driven away because suddenly I longed like never before to be held upside down in the air.

"Mrs. Wiesberg, please," the receptionist said. Because I did not see her coming I was startled and knocked my thigh into the woman next to me, who did not change her shape.

"Are you coming?" the receptionist asked. Blank stood up, put his brochure on a side table, and stood in front of me. He stood between the receptionist and me, smoothed his suit, cleared his throat several times and then held out his hand to me, the hand with the bandage on the wrist. "Come," he said, and as I took his hand I was, at least for a moment, the opposite of me.

We stood in front of the doctor's office. "Something came up at the very last-minute," I had said to the receptionist.

"My heart is racing," I said. Blank smiled. "What else should it do?" he asked.

I sat on the curb stone. Blank was standing next to me and he was silent, his hands clasped behind his back. He looked like a doorman.

In front of us people were walking along the street, buses drove past and trains rattled by and I wondered why everyone just kept walking along and driving by and rattling, why everyone simply knew what to do next. I had also asked myself that when I came home from the hospital after Jacob's death.

"I don't know what to do anymore, Blank," I said.

Blank cleared his throat, ran his fingers through his hair and crouched down in front of me. "May I take over?" he asked.

I held my hand out to him and he pulled me up. "Take over," I said.

And then Blank grew euphoric. I had never seen him like that, and I knew that some of the euphoria he displayed was explained by the fact that I did not fall into contemplation and from contemplation directly into doubt. Blank displayed a lot of euphoria in order to keep up with the amount of doubt. The whole world was full of doubt; doubt was nourished by the facts that had spoken for themselves, that had been downright garrulous, and which were now, because I had simply ignored them, insulted and vociferously silent, which can be just as challenging as any other opponent.

Blank chatted against the silence of the facts; he jumped ahead of me, he turned me around in circles and pushed me into a trolley car, which did not lead home, but to a department store. He grabbed me by the shoulders and pushed me up the stairs of the department store; it must have looked like we were staging a sparse polonaise. In the women's department he pressed me down on a stool in a dressing room, fanned out and came back with a mountain of shirts which were longer in the front than in the back, with a mountain of skirts with elastic and with bras in various sizes, whose cups you could open and close. "Those are maternity clothes," I said.

"Precisely," said Blank, holding a shirt in front of his body that was about as big as Jacob's tent.

I took the shirt from Blank's hands and folded it up. "Now just hang on a minute," I said. "We mustn't be hasty. I have to get used to the idea first."

Blank crouched down in front of me; I saw his back and the back of his head in the dressing room mirror.

"No," Blank said. He looked at me as if he was looking into my eyes for something tiny, perhaps for a hole, one that you could barely see with the naked eye. "You know," he said, "that the best thing we can do now is everything else accept hang on a minute. The best thing is to rush things."

I looked at the back of Blank's head in the mirror and checked to see whether there was perhaps another hole there. The undue haste Blank was suggesting was one that blared out that there was no turning back, and I did not know whether the reason for this blaring was my doubts or Blank's holes: the hole in Blank's upper arm, the hole in Blank's wrist.

"Okay," I said. "Let's rush it."

Blank rushed things big time. He pulled me into a furniture store to buy a baby's crib and I pulled him out again. He pulled me into a baby's clothing store, and I pulled him out of there as well; he talked about a spot in the kindergarten, which you had to take care of right away, otherwise, he had read in the newspaper, you wouldn't get a spot in the kindergarten until the child was already enrolled in school.

He pulled me into a bookstore, a bookstore with a café, fanned out, came back with a stack of literature about pregnancy and babies and sat down at one of the coffee tables. He asked me to borrow a pen from the waitress. The waitress looked at the books. "You have to buy them," she said.

Blank read and underlined. He sat hunched over the books the way, I imagined, he had once sat over the translations of his students. One and a half hours he sat there. Now and then he glanced up briefly and smiled at me. "This is all very interesting," he said.

Then we went to the checkout with seven books. The cashier packed the books in a bag, smiled at me and said: "Congratulations."

At first I did not know why she was congratulating me. Blank nudged me, the way you nudge a child who is learning to say "please" and "thank you." The only thing that could have made it worse was if he had said, "What do you say?" I said: "Thank you," thought about Armin and asked myself whether anyone else besides the cashier would congratulate me.

When you have to tell someone things that you really can't say, it's best if you can just barely see the person you need to say it to, so I did not open the door when Armin rang in the evening, but said through the intercom: "Let's take an evening stroll tonight."

"How romantic," Armin said. "But it's still a bit bright out. Can I please come in?"

"It's better if we meet at the spot, at ten," I said, as if I was describing the procedure for handing over money, and I explained to Armin how to get to the forest, which is the only forest far and wide and had always been Jacob's forest.

As Blank and I drove to the forest, Blank acted as if we had just successfully handed over money, as if we were on the way to a Caribbean beach with a travel bag full of millions. He leaned far out of the passenger window, came back inside again all disheveled, drummed his fingers on his thigh and bobbed his head, though there was no music playing. Blank turned on the radio, a music station, listened and turned it up louder. "What's that?" Blank asked. "That's nice."

"*Leaving New York*," I said. Blank sat back and listened. I looked at him out of the corner of my eye. "Should I translate it?"

Blank smiled. "No," he said. "I can speak English."

He straightened up and beamed at me. "I speak a total of seven languages. Did you know that?"

"No," I said. "I didn't know."

"Four of them, however, are dead," Blank said. He turned the music up louder, leaned back and closed his eyes.

"Blank," I said, "what am I going to do now?" Because I had no idea how I could make Armin come to terms with a pregnancy and a child. I thought maybe it would be better to keep everything a secret from Armin. I was in favor of keeping a secret; as I thought about it, if everything was intact, I would have the rest of my life to deal with Armin, and I was even more in favor of keeping a secret, as I thought about Armin's method for reducing stress. "If I tell him this," I said to Blank, "then a bungalow will no longer be enough; then he will rob a store, then he will hold up a bank, then perhaps he will start shooting and the child will have a father behind bars," and then I was one hundred percent ready for a secret, when I then also remembered Armin's grandfather, his grandfather with the pig, the grandfather with the exhausted hog, the one Armin spoke about with compassion.

The music was very loud now. "It won't work, Blank. I can't tell him this," I said.

Blank smiled at me and tapped his fingers on his thigh in time with the music. "Even a little Japanese," he said.

It was dark, but not as dark as I had hoped, and Armin had brought a picnic. He sat on the forest floor, on a tree stump next to him there was a Tupperware container, a bottle of champagne, a bag of bread and a candle.

"This is indeed a nice idea," I said, and sat down with Blank on the other side of the tree stump. Armin smiled at me.

Blank cleared his throat and said, "Now would be an opportune moment."

Armin gave me the Tupperware container. It contained slices of bread, cheese and a pork sausage spread. On the sausage were the words *From the Master's Hand*. I spread some on a piece of bread. It did not taste very good.

"It tastes like foam from a fire extinguisher," said Armin, who had also opted for the sausage. "True," I said. "But it's from the master's hand. What comes from the master's hand must somehow be good, even if we don't like it."

"An excellent lead in," Blank said. "Now."

It was quiet. There was no wind. Nothing crackled in the branches. Armin tossed the bread into the darkness behind him and covered a new piece with cheese. "So?" I asked. "How was everything today?"

"Absolutely quiet," Armin said. "Totally boring. I watched TV all day."

Armin bit into his bread, grabbed the bottle of champagne and opened it. The cork popped in the silence like a gunshot. "And how about you?"

"Now," said Blank.

"I went shopping," I said.

Armin took a swig from the bottle and held it out to me. "Thank you, but I better not," I said.

"Now," said Blank.

Armin shrugged his shoulders, placed the champagne bottle on the tree stump, opened the nutritional liquid supplement with a cigarette lighter, took a sip and leaned against the black trunk of a pine tree.

"Is Blank here, too?"

I nodded.

"Now," said Blank.

"Blank has the hiccups," I said.

Then something snapped in the branches. Armin listened. "It's not quite safe here this time of year," he said with his mouth full. "The wild boars are especially aggressive now. They've just had their young."

"Not now," Blank said. I thought about everything that I had believed would not work. About Jacob's disappearance, about Alina, about the accident, about the pregnancy, and compared to all of that what I had to say was after all laughably simple, as easy as breaking into a vacant bungalow.

"I'm pregnant," I said. I said that for the first time in my life and I would have liked to have said it differently and not like someone in an early evening soap opera, who says it as a cliff hanger, accompanied by ominous music.

"What?" Armin whispered.

"Pregnant," I said.

Armin jumped up, quicker than I have ever seen anyone jump up, and then stood upright and stared at me.

"By me?"

I nodded. "It was an accident."

At first Armin did not move. Then he slammed his hand against a tree trunk. "An accident—that's nonsense," he said. "You did this on purpose." He said that like one child who has been hit by another.

"But you're not going to have it," he said hoarsely. He explicitly said it not as a question.

I stood up. Blank stood up, too. "It looks as if I'm going to have it," I said. "But you don't have to worry about anything, if you don't want to." I took a step towards Armin and wanted to put a hand on his shoulder; he stepped back and looked like a wild animal in a trap. His eyes were wide.

"You can't foist a child on me," he cried. It sounded desperate, and as if his voice had begun to change. "You have a few screws loose." He began to pace back and forth, three steps forward, three back, as if in a reasonably spacious trap; his hands trembled. "I can't do it; you know that very well."

"Yes," I said. "I know that very well." But Armin did not hear it. "You can't foist a child on me," he said. "I don't want that yet either," I yelled and began to cry, because for the first time in my life I heard someone screaming in the forest and screams in the forest are especially terrifying, but Armin had not heard that either; he turned around and ran into the forest. Because it was dark, he immediately disappeared.

Blank shook my arm. "*Get closer to the fire; it won't get any hotter,*" he exclaimed. "Shout that out, please." I yelled it. "Ralph McQuincey," Blank yelled and shook my arm. "Ralph McQuincey," I screamed; I screamed because Armin was surely already far away. After all, he was fast.

"Just don't fuck it up," I cried even louder afterwards. My heart was beating fast, because your own screams in the forest are more terrifying than those of other people, and because the silence after screams in the forest is even more frightening than the screams themselves. The forest swallowed everything, and the forest was like a room with padded doors.

"At least not too much," I said quietly.

I turned to Blank. I had expected that Armin would go away, but I imagined his departure differently. I thought he would raise his eyebrows, tap his index finger to his forehead and say that **I** probably did have a few screws loose**,** before he turned around and slowly disappeared. I had not expected that Armin, instead of disappearing, would be almost swallowed up, and I had not expected the despair either; ultimately Armin had always been fearless; ultimately Armin loved complicated burglaries; and I had not expected cries and not a change in his voice.

I grabbed Blank's hand. Blank looked as if he expected something utterly absurd. We packed away the picnic like a short-sighted film crew with the wrong props.

"That was the last one for now," I said to Evelyn the next morning, after we had smoked in the toilet cubicle of Bengt's agency. Evelyn sat on the toilet seat.

"Have you really considered that too?" she asked, and she didn't mean the last cigarette. I shook my head.

"And the arrogant fire extinguisher—what does he say about it?"

"He doesn't think it's very good."

Evelyn sighed and talked about her sister, who brought up her daughter alone, without a man and without grandparents. "Because you're simply going crazy," Evelyn said.

I had met Evelyn's sister a year ago on Evelyn's birthday. She had sat with her one and a half year-old daughter on Evelyn's sofa. The daughter had tried to stack memory cards on the coffee table. Evelyn's sister did not only have to take care of her daughter, but the entire world. She had to make sure that her daughter did not chew up the memory cards, that she did not knock over the glasses that were left standing around, and did not grab the ashtray. Again and again Evelyn's sister moved the ashtray somewhere else, again and again someone put it back on the coffee table, and finally the daughter succeeded to reach into it. Her fingers were full of spit, so the ash stuck particularly well to them. As she climbed onto my lap, I helped her with the stacking and tried to pay attention to her and everything around her, which was also therefore very difficult because the daughter did not want attention given to everything, and

Evelyn's sister had fallen asleep in the middle of the birthday noise.

"Because you're just going crazy," Evelyn said. "Really think it over."

"The possibility always exists, however," I said. "Of going crazy, I mean." Evelyn had not been listening. She lit a cigarette. "It does you in," she said.

"I know almost nothing about Armin," I said to Blank in the evening. "I don't know where he lives; I don't even know his telephone number."

"But," said Blank, "everybody knows it. 911."

I tapped myself on the forehead. Blank said: "Maybe it is better to leave him alone for a while."

"But I could say calming things to him," I said and told Blank that once years ago I had been sitting in an airplane next to someone with a massive fear of flying, someone struck with an even more massive fear of flying than I, and I had calmed him, I had calmed everything, my own massive fear of flying, the massive fear of the airplane passengers and even the plane that had briefly lost control in the turbulence.

"A fine plan," Blank said, "but unfortunately Armin and you, I suspect, do not have the same worries."

Blank rushed bravely on. Again and again he pulled me into baby shops and I pulled him out again, and when I came home from translating one night, Blank was sitting in the kitchen, a jigsaw beside him, and had handcrafted a mobile. In a tangle of nylon threads there hung colorful little things made of wood, some of which partially resembled battered pine cones, and others plump worms. Blank's glasses had slipped down his nose; he looked at me over the frames. "A seahorse," he explained and tried to unravel the strings. He looked like he had been trying to do it for quite a while. I said to Blank that I was okay with rushing, but not with buying things for the baby before you knew that it was reasonably intact. "I can't throw out someone's things again," I said. The sentence hung motionless in the air, as if in a completely silent, nocturnal forest, and I was amazed that he agreed.

Blank looked at me for a long time, and then he began to worry. From then on he stood there every night, when I, because of the beating heart and the question of whether it would be reasonably intact, could not sleep anyway, suddenly at my bed with a book about pregnancy in his hand and because of his reading had developed a new worry. I had never seen Blank with so many worries.

"It says here," he said one night and knocked on a book about pregnancy, "that during pregnancy you should not eat rice. Did you know that?"

"I didn't know that."

"Through the rice cadmium gets into the body and the child gets cadmium poisoning. Did you know that?"

"No," I said, "I didn't know that."

"Now you know," Blank said, and looked at me anxiously.

"I don't believe it," I said after a pause, "What kind of a book is that?"

Blank clapped it shut and read the title. "*Expecting a Child. Your Companion Through Pregnancy.*"

"Can't we shake off this companion somehow?"

Blank turned the page and explained that, if you have a placental insufficiency, the child will probably be much smaller than it should be. "But I don't have a placental insufficiency," I said. "Are you sure?" Blank asked. "Relatively," I said.

"Excuse me," Blank said on another night, "but do you know if you had any alcohol recently? If you have been drinking alcohol than devastating things can happen in the brain."

"In mine?" I asked.

"No. In the baby's."

"One glass, maybe," I said. "At most. Blank, what's going on with you?"

Blank looked at me seriously. "Maybe that's enough," he said.

"A glass? For a whole brain?"

"Yes."

"I don't think so," I said.

"And why not?"

"Because it's absurd."

"That has never been an argument," Blank said, looking exhausted.

"Don't 'worry so much," I said. "We can't make ourselves crazy. We have to wait for the examination. We have to wait for everything. We probably won't know whether it's completely intact, not even when it's an adult. We have to remain calm. And above all, we have to sleep."

"You can't sleep yet."

"I could sleep very well," I said, "if you wouldn't keep barging in with this book about pregnancy. Blank, what is the matter with you? What have you got?"

Blank pushed the glasses that had slipped down back up his nose.

"Fear of flying," he said. "I have the most massive fear of flying that you can imagine."

He turned a new page. "Then, there is also the weakness in the cervix," he said.

"I have to buy something," Blank said in the morning before the examination. "Can I leave you alone for a short time?"

"Sure," I said.

"Good," Blank said, and buttoned up his suit jacket. "I'll see you later. I'll pick you up."

When Blank returned he was carrying a package the size of a shoebox, wrapped in brown paper. "Don't peek," he said, and placed it under the sink. Then we drove off.

In the humorous doctor's waiting room, Blank stared, not at the backward running clock, but at a questionnaire he had drafted that morning. There were twenty-seven questions. Blank had worked with highlighters and a red pencil. "You need to ask absolutely everything," he said.

"Everything?"

"Yes. The doctor will just have to take some time." And then I was called.

Blank continued to stand in the doorway. I sat on the treatment chair and clutched Blank's questions. The doctor looked at the monitor for a long time. What you could see there was what you would likely see if you looked into a dark forest with defective night vision goggles. "And?" she asked. "Are you looking forward to it?"

I nodded. "And your husband—is he also looking forward to it?" I nodded and accidentally crumpled Blank's list. The doctor glanced at me. Because she was looking at the monitor she missed the second nod. "Yes," I said.

The doctor looked at the screen for a while, then she said: "There's everything you need." She pointed to alleged arm and leg appendages, to an alleged head. I nodded and smiled at the doctor encouragingly, because I knew what it was like to see something that other people cannot see.

"So that means that so far everything is reasonably intact?"

"So far everything is perfectly intact," the doctor said.

"That means we can assume that it will remain intact? For the next few months, I mean?"

The doctor laughed. "Probably even longer." The nurse came in and pressed something into the doctor's hand that looked like a sales receipt. The doctor took one quick look. "And your blood count is fine, too."

"It's not lacking anything?"

"What would it be lacking?"

"I don't know," I said. "Something it needs from me. A nutrient, or a vitamin, or something."

"No," said the doctor. "It has everything it needs." And then she strapped an instrument around my belly. "Listen," she said." Those are heart beats."

I thought of Blank's moveable heart and whether anyone had been able to hear its movability. The heart beats were very loud. "It sounds like a broken dishwasher," I said.

"It does," the doctor said. "All hearts sound like defective dishwashers."

I turned around. Blank stood there, his head leaning against the door frame, one hand in his pocket, one hand on his chest, and smiled.

"It's intact," I said as we sat in the car. I whispered it, because it was a breakthrough discovery. "Blank! It's intact. It sounds like a broken dishwasher, but it's supposed to," I whispered. "It's intact; isn't that incredible? Who would have thought it? Would you have thought it?"

Blank nodded. I took his hand and held it. I held it a long time and then pressed it to my mouth. "Please don't ever go away," I whispered behind his extended hand. "And I promise you that I'll never go away."

The pharmacist was wearing the sweater with the screensaver pattern again and had a good memory. "Nutritional liquid supplement?" he asked. "No," I said. "Band-Aids, please. For medium-sized injuries."

The pharmacist brought back a small package.

"I'm afraid that's not enough," said Blank, who stood next to me without looking at me. "It's been getting worse lately."

"It would be best if I take two more packs," I said. The pharmacist brought back two more. "Why do you need so many?"

I had been afraid he would ask that. "My son falls down all the time," I said. "I can't keep up with putting bandages on him anymore. He's ... he's a little ..."

"Bully," Blank said.

"He's a real little bully."

"Kids!" The pharmacist smiled sympathetically. "We have three."

"Oh."

"Like I always say: Little kids, little worries. Big kids, big worries."

"Oh."

"Our youngest is already enrolled in school."

"Oh."

The pharmacist glanced at my stomach. "And now is there a little brother or sister on the way?"

I stared at him. "How did you know that?"

"You've grown a little more voluptuous," he said. "If I may be permitted to say so. It can't all be because of the nutritional liquid supplement."

"How can people tell?"

The pharmacist folded his hands over his belly. "From the sparkle in your eyes," he said solemnly. "The sparkle in the eyes of an expectant mother."

I looked at Blank in shock. "Do I have a sparkle in my eyes?"

Blank shook his head. "Not particularly remarkable."

"Oh yes, have you," the pharmacist said.

At home, I ripped open the package of Band-Aids and began to bandage Blank. Because we were not talking about the holes, I asked, "Is this voluptuousness very conspicuous already?" Blank nodded.

Lately my blouses felt strained, my pants did not fit anymore, but I thought the voluptuousness was only marginally true, because Blank's physical changes were much more disturbing. Blank was anything but voluptuous; Blank now had a hole the size of an orange above his right knee and another one, and this one was particularly bad, in his left cheek. Blank looked injured.

"Does it have something to do with the baby?" I asked.

"Growing voluptuous? That's quite obvious."

I knelt down in front of him and took four of the Band-Aids out of the package to patch up his leg.

"No, I mean your ...these spots."

Blank looked down at me. "How so?"

"I just thought," I said, "that maybe you think something will replace you. I just thought. That would be ... well, that would indeed," I said, and realized how hot I was—hot and dizzy. "That would be very wrong."

"No, no. That's not it," Blank said. "I don't know where it's coming from. I have no control over it."

"Would you turn around, please?" I asked, as if Blank was at a fitting; as if I was a gentlemen's tailor.

He turned around. I stuck two bandages behind the bend in his knees.

"Do I have any effect? Please turn around again."

Blank turned around again. I stuck a second bandage on his kneecap, then a third, to be safe.

"No," Blank said.

I looked up at him. He took a deep breath and swallowed.

"I would really like to stay," he said. "I would really like to get to know it."

When we met Alina, I was not expecting it. We met her on her way to the post office. It was absurd, because Alina lived somewhere else. She was coming towards us; I recognized her immediately, even though I had only seen her once. I had often wondered if and when I would meet Alina. Sometimes I had told Blank that we would surely meet her today, but we had never met her, and Blank finally said: "She probably doesn't really exist."

I was prepared; I had been thinking about what I would say to Alina. I had planned to ask her why she and Jacob had not said anything to me much earlier, and instead had left me in the dark; whether or not she knew, I wanted to ask Alina, that ambiguity is an intolerable situation, that you sit in the darkness as if in a bathtub, in which the water has grown cold and from which one does not come out; I had planned to demand her explanations, because I believed that explanations made not only dental care less painful, and I wanted to demand that she tell me how Jacob had been on the morning before his accident; whether they had been together on that morning; whether she had been the last person he had seen before the accident and what they had talked about. I had planned to interrogate Alina.

Alina was very thin and very blond. She wore a summer dress; she looked like someone in an advertisement for something expensive that will never go on sale. Alina stopped in front of us. Blank put his arm around my shoulder. "Hello," Alina said, smiling.

I noticed that tears sprang to my eyes and I tried to blink them away; tears do not fit into an interrogation, at least not on the part of the interrogator. Blinking them away did not work, mainly because I had to think about Armin, how, when the door of the room at the guest house finally opened, he had said to McQuincey that for days and nights he had done nothing else except wait for him.

"Hello," I said and wanted to say more, all sorts of things not fit for an interrogation, and then I felt sick. I leaned against the wall of a house. Blank reached for my hand.

"Thank you for the flowers," I said to Alina, then I threw up on the curb; I threw up my entire breakfast right next to Alina's shoes. Alina held me by the shoulders.

"Sorry," I said and wiped the back of my hand over my mouth.

Blank stood behind Alina. Their heads were side by side; Alina looked worried. "You mustn't take that personally," I said, trying to smile.

"Are you pregnant?" Alina asked. I nodded.

"Congratulations."

"Thanks," I said. I looked at Alina's face. It was very bright, her skin almost transparent at her temples you could see fine blue veins. After a while Alina said: "You mustn't take it personally, either."

"What?"

Alina took my hand. You could hardly feel her weight. "He used to say only nice things about you," she said, and because Jacob had said only nice things about me, I immediately felt sick again.

Alina took her hand out of mine and patted me on the arm. "Good luck," she said, and left.

"Hey," I exclaimed.

Alina turned around, waved at me and moved on. She had an almost graceful walk. Blank and I watched her.

I thought about my wedding, about the jetty where I had been lying with Jacob and Evelyn and where Evelyn, because she had lived with a Buddhist, had said that every encounter of a person with another person is the encounter of an empty boat with another empty boat. That had seemed wrong to me. Instead, I thought that there were only ever encounters between fully loaded boats, that were swept together and then the carelessly stacked and poorly lashed together cargo got all mixed up and then the essentials always fell overboard; but now, as I watched Alina, I thought suddenly and for a short time, that perhaps you only encountered empty boats, even if you could see with your own eyes that they were loaded with junk and precious things; perhaps, I thought, nobody in the world can believe his eyes; perhaps all boats are empty, even if everyone swears that they are jam-packed.

"She's a ghost," Blank said.

"She's an empty boat," I said. "And me, too. And you, too."

Blank smiled and looked down at me. "You seem pretty full to me," he said.

Because so far everything was intact, because the heart sounded as prescribed like a broken dishwasher, I no longer pulled Blank out of the baby stores.

He had made a list of the essentials; the essentials were a total of thirty-two things. We bought a baby bed and the thirty-one other things, and placed the baby bed under Blank's tangled mobile. I had hung up the mobile after the doctor had said that everything necessary was all there. "Normally it's the other way around," Blank said as we assembled the bed.

"What is usually the other way around?"

Blank was cleaning his glasses. "Normally you have the bed first, and then hang the mobile above it."

"Normally," I said and placed a bag full of tiny clothes in the bed. "What do you really think?" Blank asked. "Is it a girl or a boy? I think it's a girl."

"Me, too," I said. "Blank, there's another one."

"No. Where?"

"On your shin. There. On the left."

Because I could think of nothing else, I started to cook. The holes were numerous, so I came up with the idea that perhaps it would help to eat something. "Or maybe astronaut food?" I asked, and Blank said, "Please, no."

I prepared vitamin-rich and high calorie things for Blank, vegetable casseroles with lots of cheese, potato gratin with lots of cream; I mixed banana shakes and smeared bread with Camembert. Blank ate everything; I also ate everything, because I also had to eat something else besides artichoke hearts. I kept eating artichoke hearts lately, artichoke hearts and marzipan, by the pound. I had not liked either of them before.

"That's normal," Blank said. "And I would like to have a little of this wonderful gratin."

"Do you notice anything?" I asked after a week, when we were sitting down at dinner. Blank took another wedge of processed cheese and looked at me quizzically. "I mean, do you feel heavier? Or thicker? Impenetrable?"

Blank looked down at himself. "No," he said.

Nothing helped. Nothing helped, and one morning when I wanted to wake Blank, when I walked to his sofa with a banana shake in my hand, touched him on the arm and said: "Blank, good morning," Blank did not wake up.

I put the banana shake on the floor and stroked his arm, cautiously at first, then harder. "Blank?"

Blank did not respond. My heart began to race; I put a hand on my stomach and tried to calmly stroke it lightly with my hands, because I knew that if your heart starts racing when you are pregnant, the other heart will start racing, too. I leaned over and shook both of Blank's shoulders. "Blank," I cried, and it sounded like my voice was changing. Blank took a deep breath, opened his eyes and looked at me in shock. "What's the matter? Has something happened? "

I exhaled. "Thank God," I said. "I thought you were dead."

Blank giggled. It was the first and only time that I heard him giggle.

When I came home at night from translating and greeted Blank, who stood at the living room window with his arms folded behind his back, looking out, when I said, "Good evening," and said I had to go out again soon because I had forgotten to buy potatoes and bananas and artichoke hearts, Blank said nothing.

I went to him and tapped him on the shoulder. He turned his head towards me; his face was pale. "It can't be delayed any longer," he said.

I dropped my bag. It did not help to eat anything, nothing helped, and the idea that all boats, as full as they seemed, were basically empty, didn't help a bit. Blank cleared his throat. "I have to ask you something." I nodded.

"Could you imagine coming with me?"

I stood beside him at the window; we looked out into the pitch-dark garden.

"Sure," I said. "When?"

"Tonight," Blank said.

I picked up my bag and stroked Blank's shoulder.

"See you later," I said. "I'll pick you up."

The house was a terraced house very close to me, an old building, tall and white. We were standing outside the front door; it was shortly before midnight and very cold. I turned up my collar. Because my own no longer fit, I wore Jacob's coat, I had rolled up the sleeves, and then it was time. I glanced at the nameplates. At the top, in large letters, as if it were the most natural thing in the world, it said: BLANK.

"You lived here the entire time," I said. "Yes," said Blank. "The entire time."

I shook my head. "I've gone by this house a million times. Where were you all that time?"

"Inside, I suppose," he said. "Inside or in the classroom..." Blank looked nervous, as if it was necessary to break in somewhere, to bring back something that did not belong to him. I looked up at the house. "We haven't thought this through very well," I said. "How are we going to do this? I won't be able to knock. Will I?"

"She won't invite you in," Blank said. "She's always very skeptical of strangers. Of strange women, I mean."

"I could make up something."

"Like what?"

"I could say that I moved in next door and I forgot my key. And that my husband isn't reachable and won't be home until later. She won't make me stand out in the cold."

"She'll call Mr. Metzler, the neighbor, so he'll let you in," Blank said. "My wife is very skeptical."

Blank looked at me, puzzled. Blank, who otherwise always had lists and plans, now stood there with empty hands and buried them in his pockets. In front of the house was a huge chestnut; its crown was the same height as the top floor. I had a bag of artichoke hearts with me and took one out. "I could try to climb up there."

"Don't you dare," Blank said indignantly. He looked up again at the house, for a long time, as if he awaited a rope ladder, and then at the tips of his shoes. "It was a stupid idea," he said at last. "And it's not so bad; it's enough, if you're waiting for me downstairs. Then you are indeed nearby."

I grabbed Blank's arm. "No," I said. "That's not enough. I'll back you up. I'll stay close to you. And I know how." I pulled my phone out of my coat pocket and dialed the number that everyone knows. It rang twice, and then a male voice said: "Fire department. What's happened?"

"Good evening," I said. "My cat is stuck in a treetop."

"I understand. Animal in distress."

"Exactly. Animal in distress. Louisenstraße 12. Could you send someone?"

"Are you sure that there isn't any other way?"

"What other kind of way?"

"A ladder?"

"You mean a normal ladder?"

"Yes. Ladder. Normal."

"It won't reach. I mean, mine won't reach. I already tried it."

"Okay," said the fireman and was about to hang. "Stop!" I cried, a little too loudly. "Can you tell me if Mr. Armin Golling, by any chance, is on duty?"

"Golling? He's here."

I held the phone to my chest and stared at Blank.

"He really is a fireman." Blank nodded and pointed at my phone. "Hello? Hello!" the fireman yelled to my chest.

"Sorry," I said into the phone. "Then could you possibly please send Mr. Golling? He got the cat out of the tree for me once before. She's a real little bully. I had a good experience with Mr. Golling that time. He's very sensitive. At least with animals."

"Listen," the fireman said. "This isn't a radio show you can just call up to request your favorite song. Goodbye."

"Wait!" I exclaimed.

"What for?"

"It is, by the way, totally sufficient if Mr. Golling comes alone," I said. "You don't have to bother about it. He really doesn't need to bring anyone. The cat ... the cat is very small."

"My people never go out on a call alone."

"But maybe it's even better if he comes alone," I said and looked at Blank helplessly. "If there are so many strange people, the animal might be frightened and fall from tree." And the fireman hung up.

"Armin is really a fireman," I said. Blank had not heard me. He looked up, up to the fifth floor, as if there was something sitting there, high at the top of the gutter that was invincible.

"*Do not think about winning, but think about how not to lose*," I said.

"Karate?"

I nodded.

"So you're coming along?" Blank asked. "You'll be nearby?"

"Yes," I said. "I'll be nearby. And afterwards I'll pick up you up right here."

"Then I'll go now."

"Yes. See you later."

"See you later."

Blank disappeared. I sat on the steps in front of the door, ate one artichoke heart and asked myself what Blank would say to his wife, if he had made a list, a list with questions or with answers, sorted by relevance. Then a huge fire truck came around the corner, with a ladder that looked like a folded crane. I stood up. Armin drove; a fellow fireman sat in the passenger seat. The truck stopped, Armin opened the door, jumped out and ran up to me.

"So it was you, then," he said. "I should have guessed. Holger said that someone totally loony called. Someone who said I would be sensitive to animals." Armin looked at my breasts. "You've changed," he said.

I looked at Armin as if he was an apparition. "You're a fireman."

"And what a fireman," Armin said. "There's something I really need to tell you. There is something really big that happened. And, listen, if this is because of the issue..."

"No," I said. "It's about Blank." And I explained to Armin that I had to go quickly to the fifth floor In order to assist Blank from the window.

"Do you want to break in there or what?"

"No," I said. "It's just about being nearby. So one can say afterwards that one has seen it, that one was there, you know?"

"No."

"*It's about the liberation of the mind,*" I said.

Armin looked at me, astonished. "Karate Rule number six," he said.

"Precisely."

Armin sighed. "Very well." He took his radio from his belt. "Frank, the animal is in the top of the tree," he said into the device, even though Frank was in earshot. "I'm taking the owner up with me."

"Is that necessary?" Frank asked over the radio. "Can't she wait down here?"

"It's difficult," said Armin and looked at me. "The animal is ... the animal isn't very good with men."

We climbed into the ladder cage. Frank raised the ladder up. The house lights went on; residents stuck out their heads.

"Is it on fire?" asked someone whose living room we rode past. "No," I said. "Don't worry. Only a cat."

Armin grinned. *"It's about the liberation of the mind,"* he said, but the resident had fortunately retracted his head again.

I had no idea that I suffered from vertigo. Now I knew it and made up my mind to ask Blank whether he had found in his pregnancy book anything about a pregnancy-related fear of heights.

"Stop," I said when we were at a fifth floor window. "Stop," Armin said into his radio.

"We're not even at the tree," Frank said. "I know," Armin said. "We have to approach the animal slowly."

Frank laughed. "You really are sensitive with animals," he said and held onto the ladder.

I held my face close to the window. Behind it was dark. I saw an unmade bed, a closet, a huge ceiling lamp. "Further to the left," I said. The next window was right next to the top of the tree.

"Now a little further to the left," Armin said into his device.

"I admire your courage," Frank said, and moved the ladder to the left.

The kitchen window was half obscured by a lace curtain, which also hid Armin and me up to the tips of our noses.

"Tell him that he should leave it just like this."

Armin pressed the intercom button on his radio.

"Perfect, Frank," he said.

You could hear nothing but music, which was muffled outside but loud enough to drown out the sound of the ladder. The kitchen was very large. At the table in the middle sat a woman and a man. The woman was undoubtedly Blank's wife; she looked exactly the way Blank had described her. She had pinned up her black curly hair; she wore a bright, dotted blouse, and a tight skirt that hung just over the knee. She had placed her left leg on the empty chair, a round leg in a nylon tights; Blank had said that she was proud of her legs because they were still smooth and without a single varicose vein. Her high-heeled shoe had come loose. It rested on its toe. "Looks good," Armin said. "For her age."

I nodded. Blank's wife smoked a cigarette and listened to the man, who sat across from her. When she laughed, she threw her head back, and only when she laughed could you see her age up to this point, the wrinkles, which quickly spread across her face.

"Is that Blank's widow?" Armin whispered, and I was shocked at the word; I thought of her only as Blank's wife, never as Blank's widow. I also thought of myself only as Jacob's wife, as Jacob's wife abandoned by Jacob, and never as Jacob's widow.

"Yes."

"And who is that guy?"

"No idea," I whispered. The man sitting across from her was about sixty, tall and broad; he wore a light suit, and his gray hair was slicked back and shiny. He leaned over the table and smoked a cigarillo; the smoke he blew narrowly missed Mrs. Blank, and he was apparently saying funny things, because Blank's wife threw her head back often.

On the table were two empty plates, two glasses, and one bottle of wine; the kitchen was full of cigarette smoke. I wondered if Blank had selected the table and chairs during his lifetime; if he had bought the glasses, maybe even the wine.

"Perhaps the gentlemen's tailor or one of his customers," Armin said. "It's not exactly the best time that your Blank has picked."

"Maybe it's only a relative."

"You don't even believe that yourself," said Armin. "Who is he then?"

Blank was nowhere to be seen. "I don't know," I whispered.

Armin coughed and tapped me on the shoulder. "I have to tell you something."

I turned to face him. "It's okay," I said. "You really don't have to worry about anything."

"No, no. That's not it." Armin put his hands on my shoulders and suddenly he had tears in his eyes. "What is it?"

"It's the big thing that happened. I have…" Armin said hoarsely, "I rescued someone. For the first time in my life I saved a person's life."

"Really?"

"Really," Armin said, smiled and wiped a tear from his cheek with the back of his hand. "A real person, from a real burning apartment. A ninety-two year old woman. She was a little confused and thought in the middle of April it was New Year's Eve, and set off firecrackers. In the apartment. I rescued her, and her dog—I also rescued him. At the last second. From a sea of flames."

"A sea of flames?"

"Well, a medium-size fire. But enormous."

"That's fantastic," I said and hugged Armin. "Congratulations." I let him go, but Armin didn't let me go. I looked up at him. His eyes were shining; he beamed.

"And now I'll rescue you," he said.

"That's nice of you, Armin, but I don't need to be rescued," I said, squirming out of his embrace and glancing into the kitchen. Blank was still not there. Armin smiled at me. "But," he said, patting belly, "with the little fireman here, we'll manage it somehow."

I looked at my belly and at Armin's caressing hand, and I felt sick both of Armin's caress and the idea of a tiny, uniformed mustachioed fireman who was camped in my belly and who I somehow had to manage with Armin.

"We'll have to see about that," I said, like a dentist speaking to someone who has assured him their teeth are okay, and then I looked back into the apartment, and suddenly Blank was standing in the kitchen door.

"There he is," I said. Blank glanced out the window. I nodded to him like someone standing on a ten-meter diving board for the first time. He looked at the stove that was standing right beside the door. One of the front burners glowed; Blank switched it off. He continued to stand in front of the stove; in his black suit covered with bandages, he looked as if he could not move forwards or backwards.

"Now," I said. I said it too Blank, who could not hear me. "Now."

Blank took one step into the kitchen, then another. Finally, he stood directly in front of his wife. She reached for the cigarette on the table. She looked in Blank's direction, the way one often looks into the void during a conversation, to listen, to think, and, without looking at the box, fingered out a cigarette, then looked away and at the lighter, lit the cigarette, leaned back and smiled at the man sitting across from her, who said amusing things and never had been a relative.

Blank looked at me. I nodded. Blank walked even closer to his wife, hesitated briefly, touched her shoulder and pulled back his hand, as if he had received an electric shock.

His wife nodded and laughed at her guest. I dropped the bag with the artichoke hearts. An artichoke heart fell through the mesh of the cage. I watched it; it fell incredibly far and a long time passed before it silently landed on the asphalt. Armin looked at me from the side.

"What's the matter?" he asked. "Have you seen a ghost?"

I had counted on everything. On the fact that Blank's wife would be frightened; that she would be terribly frightened; that she would rejoice; that she would weep, from joy or fright; that she would try to chase Blank; that she would ask him to stay; but not on this.

"She can't see him," I said.

Blank stretched out his hand again, and again he touched his wife's shoulder. Then he crouched down next to her chair and stroked her back. Blank's wife drew on her cigarette and grasped her neck with the other hand, as if her head was suddenly heavy. Blank stood up, held his face close to her and said something; he said many things close to her face, and the fact that I was not able to hear it was obvious, but that Blank's wife was not able to hear it was unbearable; Blank's wife brushed her fingers lightly over her eyelids and in the process she touched Blank's bandaged cheek, without realizing it. She smiled, took her leg off the chair, bent far across the table and kissed her guest. She kissed him for a long time.

"Shit," Armin said. Blank had receded, and now stood, as motionless as a statue, at the head of the kitchen table. Then he reached with trembling hands into the inside pocket of his suit and pulled out a pen. He took a sheet from a stack of papers on the telephone table. He reached for the sheet without looking; I had to remind myself that Blank knew his way around in this apartment, that he knew it by heart. He turned around, put the paper on the dresser and wrote something on it. I saw his bent back. Then Blank turned to the window and held the paper high above his head.

" BUT YOU SEE ME, CAN YOU SEE ME?" it said there in shaky capital letters, and because he had turned the sign towards his wife, I did not know whether YOU meant his wife and her guest or me, so I did not know if I should nod or shake my head. I pointed to my chest. "Yes," Blank said. You couldn't hear it, but you could see it, and I began to nod violently, more violently than I had ever nodded in my life. Armin looked at me. "You have to nod, too," I said. 'Please, you have to nod," and Armin nodded too; he nodded so much that he had to hold his helmet.

Blank lowered the paper. Armin's radio began to hiss. "What's going on with the cat?" Frank asked. "It's not easy," Armin said. "The animal is totally distraught."

"I'm not surprised, with that owner," Frank said. "Tell me, are you having fun up there? Do you have something going on with her?"

I leaned over the radio, without taking my eyes off the kitchen. "No," I said.

"Yes, indeed," Armin said quietly.

"Well, speed things up, damn it," Frank said. Blank stared at his wife, who stood up, smiling, and with swaying hips walked towards her guest. She walked past Blank, who drew in his belly and lifted his shoulders to avoid contact. She sat on her guest's lap; the guest smiled and took out his cigarillo; she wrapped her arms around her guest's neck and kissed him.

"You have to go now," I whispered, "Go now, please."

"Is he still there?" Armin asked. I nodded.

"Listen," said Frank, after a while from the radio, "I'm bringing you down now, with or without the cat. It's quitting time."

"Just a second," Armin said, and Frank said, "I'm counting to ten."

Blank now turned away abruptly, went back to the telephone table, took the stack of paper and sat down with it at the table, on the chair where his wife had just been sitting. He coughed, as he always coughed when something was important, with his fist in front of his mouth; he straightened his back, looked again at his wife, who was at the other end of the table kissing her guest, removed the cap from the pen and began to write. He wrote quickly, without thinking and as if he was taking notes, as if someone was dictating something to him.

Blank wrote like someone possessed and did not look up. Blank's wife and her guest, who had pushed his hand under her blouse in such a way that you could see a section of her snow-white back, were still kissing. Finally she got up; Blank's wife took her guest by the hand, she walked past Blank, who did not look up, and out of the kitchen.

"We can't leave," I said to Armin and Frank said: "Ten." I waved my arms in front of the kitchen window. Blank finally looked up. I gave him an inquiring look and pointed down with my thumb. Blank looked at me, preoccupied, as if I had disturbed him while correcting a translation, and nodded.

I picked up the bag with the artichoke hearts. We rode down. Again I felt the fear of heights, which in the meantime had been forgotten; again residents leaned from the windows. "What's going on with the cat?" one asked.

"Escaped," Armin said.

"What's going on with the cat?" I whispered as we climbed out of the gondola, Frank climbed out of the truck and approached us.

Armin grinned. "No idea, but it's yours."

"And? Where is the cat?" Frank asked.

"It was, to be precise, a parakeet," I said. Frank drew his eyebrows together. "You said cat. We wouldn't have come out because of one parakeet."

"Exactly," I said.

"Look here," Frank said. "That's fraud. That can really be expensive."

"But it was a beloved parakeet," I said. "And now he has escaped. That's punishment enough. Right, Armin?"

"It's still fraud," Frank said.

"Now don't get excited, Frank," Armin said and put one arm around me and one around Frank. "The truth is: This woman is crazy about me. She just confessed it to me. And she wanted to tell me in a place connected to me, with my job, I mean. Right, Sweetie Pie?"

"Yes," I said, and coughed, "Sweetie Pie."

Armin kissed me on the mouth. "She said that she loves me and wants to be the mother of my children. Isn't that sweet?"

"Sweet," Frank said dubiously. "Can we go now?"

Frank went to the truck and climbed inside. Armin pulled a postcard from the inside pocket of his uniform jacket and held it out to me. "Translate it quickly," he said.

The postcard showed a beach at sunset. The words *Heer lijk Zandvoort* were written in a curved font in the middle of the sun. I turned the card over. "Dear Armin, Congratulations," I translated. "That is great news. I will write more soon. I have a lot to do right now with my ... with my lifesaving certificate. Your old friend, Ralph." I turned the card over again. "He's really a lifeguard."

"Sure," said Armin. "Let's go," Frank shouted through the window.

"Now you can truly save people together," I said. Armin shook his head ruefully. "There are no fires in the sea." He smiled at me. "You see, he thinks it's good."

"Of course," I said. "That was truly heroic."

"Do you think so?"

"Armin, let's shake a leg," Frank said.

"Of course. Everyone finds something heroic."

Armin grinned. "I didn't write him anything about the fire. He congratulated me about the business over the baby."

"Oh," I said, "but how did McQuincey know about that?"

"I told him. On the phone," Armin said.

"What did you say?"

"Armin Dad," said Armin, proudly. "Hello Ralph. Armin Dad."

I wondered whether Armin had wanted to tell McQuincey that he was going to be a father, or that he was as good as dead; presumably it had been the same thing at the time of his call.

"And what did he say?"

"He laughed. Very loudly. I had to hold the telephone away."

"Have a nice evening, then," Frank cried, started the engine and drove off.

"Thank you, Armin," I said. "Thank you very much."

Armin undid the buckle of his fire helmet, swung it like a top hat and bowed deeply. I jammed the bag with the artichoke hearts under my arm and applauded.

"You're welcome," Armin said, ran behind the fire engine, jumped up, grabbed hold of the overhanging ladder, kicked his legs out in the air, pulled himself up, sat down on the ladder and waved.

I sat on the steps outside the front door and waited for Blank. It had grown colder; I rolled down the sleeves of Jacob's coat so that my hands disappeared inside them, wrapped my arms around my body and wondered whether a person, when a person froze during pregnancy, just froze themselves or also the other one. I pulled up the coat collar, leaned my head against the plaster of the wall and closed my eyes.

When I opened them again, Blank was sitting beside me. His pointed knees in the black suit pants stuck in the air; he had his arms folded across his stomach. I put my arm around his shoulder, which must have looked strange, because Blank's shoulders were much higher than mine. "How are you?" I asked.

"She left the stove on again," Blank said. He tried to smile but could not. He paused, and then he said: "She didn't see me. She didn't see me or hear me."

"I know," I said, stroking Blank on the back. "I do. I was there. I saw it."

"I'm not there anymore," Blank said. "But the gentlemen's tailor is there, and I couldn't do anything about it. And even when I was still there, there was nothing I could do about it. Even when I was there, I could do as little about it as a ghost."

Leaving would have helped, I thought, but it was better not to say it, because it wasn't a helpful phrase; it was just as helpful as the business about the empty boats, that were fully loaded, since they could be as empty as they wanted, and Blank said: "I should have walked out. I should have just walked out."

I leaned my head against his shoulder. "Can you really be a hundred percent sure?"

Blank smiled. "Of course," he said.

"What did you write down in there?"

Blank reached into the inside pocket of his suit and retrieved a few folded pages. "I wrote to you," he said. "A list."

He held the pages out to me and pulled them back again.

"You have to promise me that you will read this later," he said, and I tried not to imagine what Blank meant by later.

"I promise," I lied.

"You're lying."

"Yes."

Blank put the letter back into the inner pocket of his suit.

"But you intend to give that to me?" I asked. "You won't forget it?"

"I promise," Blank said.

We did not talk about it, and although and because we did not talk about it, I knew that there was only a little time left. Because I wanted to spend it completely with Blank, I called Bengt, held my nose and said I had a pregnancy-related feverish cold. "I had no idea that you were pregnant," Bengt said. "I thought the weight gain was due to emotional overeating."

"No," I said.

"Well then, congratulations. Was that going on while Jacob was still alive?"

I let go of my nose. "What?"

"The thing with the other man."

I held my nose again. "Bengt," I said. "Bengt. What kind of a name it that?"

"What?"

"No," I said. "It was not going on."

"Then that's just fine," said Bengt. "To be cheated on—you don't wish that on anybody."

"You're right," I said. "You don't wish that on anybody."

Blank came into the living room, sat down next to me on the sofa and crossed his legs together.

Bengt sighed. "And does that mean that I have to worry about a maternity leave replacement now or what?"

I acted as if I had to sneeze, and sneezed very loudly into the middle of the receiver. "That's exactly what it means, Bengt," I said, hung up and let go of my nose.

Blank smiled at me. "Do we want to clean up a little?" he asked.

On the one hand, Blank acted as if he was preparing everything for a long journey, and on the other hand, as if we had just moved in together.

He cleaned and swept, even behind the shelves and cabinets. He scrubbed the floors and cleaned the mirror, the refrigerator and all the lights; the apartment was cleaner than it had ever been before. I asked him why he did it, and Blank said: "You shouldn't do these things anymore, in your state."

I handed Blank sponges, dusters, brooms and dustpans.

"I'm very sorry," I said as Blank hung upside down in the bathtub and scrubbed away the dirty marks around the drain, "about all that with your wife. That was terrible."

Blank paused. "She didn't see me," he said into the bathtub. Then he scrubbed. "You will be very inflexible, you know. Shortly before the end you probably won't even be able to tie your shoes."

"How do you really know all that? From the books about pregnancy?"

Blank came up and wiped the back of his hand on his forehead. "I also have a child," he said, and then his upper body disappeared into the bathtub again.

"I didn't know. You never told me."

"The child is living in Japan," Blank said. "We've had very little contact in recent years. We called on birthdays and at Christmas. We don't have much ... we don't have very much in common. At least not in the last twenty years. But it was different when it was small."

"How old is your child?"

Blank came up again. "My child is twenty-four."

"Is it a woman?"

""A man," Blank said.

"Why did you have so little contact?"

Blank scratched his head. "It worked out that way. And it's not so bad as long as I know that things are going well for him. Things are going well for him. He simply lives in a different world."

"What's he doing?"

Blank cleared his throat. "He's a dentist."

"What?"

"Really."

I laughed. "That's true. Dentists live in a completely different world."

I thought for a moment about asking Blank whether he had been there at the birth of his son. "Incidentally, I have a little something for you," Blank said, put the sponge on the edge of the bathtub and went into the kitchen. "Come here," he said.

I went into the kitchen. Blank took the box out from under the sink, that he had procured before the doctor's examination. In it was a pair of shoes without laces or Velcro, as well as a long shoehorn. "They're very convenient, especially in the months when you're inflexible," Blank said. This is a parting gift, I thought. "That's very nice of you," I said.

Blank suggested rearranging the furniture. "We could move this shelf somewhere else, because it looks a little lost," he said.

"That's what Armin said, too," I said, and we moved the shelf to a place where, Blank thought, it looked a little less lost.

"Blank, the shoes, if I may ask—how did you buy them?"

Blank turned red; I had never seen him blush. "That's a little embarrassing to me," he said. "And I have to say, I've never done something like that before. And I will also never do it again. But as you can imagine, I had no other choice."

"You stole them?"

Blank nodded.

"I'll tell Armin about that. He will be very proud of you."

"Please don't," Blank said seriously. "It's really embarrassing to me."

We knew that this was the last time, and I wasn't sure that we should spend it cleaning and rearranging, but maybe un-dramatic cleaning and rearranging was the best that one could do, but maybe the best thing was also to speak dramatic sentences, simply because, in contrast to the time prior to any others, abrupt farewells give us the opportunity to do so, because you saw this farewell coming, because Blank's farewell was a foreseeable farewell, the first foreseeable farewell in my life.

Blank dribbled scouring cleaner on a sponge and cleaned the sink. I watched him.

Goodbye, I thought.

You have saved my life, I thought.

You are the best thing that ever happened to me, I thought.

It will be very painful to let you go, I thought.

I love you, I thought.

I will never forget you, I thought.

"The flamingo, incidentally, would be better right next to the window," Blank said. He did not turn around; he cleaned the sink.

I ran into the bathroom. I felt sick, not because I was pregnant and not because everything I had tentatively thought had sounded like the lyrics of a karate movie song, but because all of this was true, because it would be painful, and because, as opposed to a dental treatment, no one could say how long it would be painful, only why.

When I returned, Blank had repositioned the flamingo.

"Do you like that?"

"Yes. Maybe we should sit down for a while. What do you think?"

Blank looked at me and ran his hand across his forehead. "Better not," he said. "We must not stop now."

I paused and looked at Blank.

He rubbed his forehead. His hand trembled slightly. "Because otherwise I'd be very unhappy," he said.

"Good," I said. "We won't stop." And I followed Blank into the bedroom.

"The baby bed is still not right," Blank said. It was placed at the foot of the bed, that was now just my bed. We cleared out the wardrobe and pushed it out the bedroom into the hallway, so the baby bed could go next to my bed.

In the mountain of things that now lay in front of the hall closet, there were still some of Jacob's things. I knelt down and made a pile of Jacob's things and one of mine.

Jacob's pile was relatively small. Because my tops no longer fit, I had taken all of his shirts. They didn't fit, but it didn't matter, they were better than the maternity tops that Blank and I had bought in a hurry; with the exception of one top we had not taken a close look and therefore had not noticed that on the fronts, at belly height, pictures and sentences were printed: a bear with a heart in his hand which said *Mama;* a comic baby sucking a pacifier; *Here Comes Trouble* or *Made With Love*.

I took a bag from the kitchen and packed Jacob's stuff inside; the bag was just big enough. Blank was in the bedroom.

"I could take the rest of Jacob's things to the charity collection bin," I yelled.

"Yes," Blank yelled back. "That's a good idea."

I looked at the bright green bag. It was stretched to the breaking point.

"Maybe I'll keep it," I yelled. Blank came out of the bedroom. He had a broom in his hand, with the bristles turned up; it was full of cobwebs. "We can simply drive to the bin and then see whether you want to throw the stuff in or not," he said. "We can drive back and forth several times."

Blank was serious about this, I knew, that he would drive back and forth with me several times, again and again to the collection bin and again and again back, with Jacob's stuff in the trunk until I had finally thrown it into the collection bin or ultimately did not, and in the end it would be a good thing, as it were, it would be good to throw the bag in, and just as good to bring it home again.

"It will take too much time," I said. "I would rather leave it right here." I took the bag, stood on tiptoe and tried to place it in the cupboard, but I was too short. Blank stood beside me and pushed it up. Then he went back into the bedroom. I took a few steps back. The bulging bag lay in the cabinet, like a lonely, much too big and much too thick caterpillar in distress, who, in contrast to all its relatives, despite the greatest concentration did not want to pass through a pupal stage.

I went to Blank in the bedroom. The mobile hung disentangled above the baby bed. Blank had moved away a chest of drawers and cleaned behind the baseboard. His glasses slipped down his sweaty nose again and again; he pushed them up with the back of his hand. "You really don't have to do that," I said.

He looked up at me briefly. "I'm very happy to do it."

I sat on my bed. In front of it, between the things that Blank had swept out from under the bed, lay one of Armin's knee socks. I picked it up. It was now evening, and dusk. Outside it began to rain. The rain wasted no time drizzling; it poured down without a prelude. The window was open, the wind moved the mobile, and the rain drowned out the quiet clacking of small wooden pieces against small wooden pieces. I turned Armin's sock in my hands, wrapped it around one wrist, and then the other.

"I miss him beyond all measure," I said and I hoped Blank would not come any closer, that he would not sit by me, because otherwise it would pour down without a prelude. Blank looked over at me. "I know," he said, stood up and sat next to me. I wrapped my arms around his neck, and it began to pour. Blank pulled my head to his chest.

"And I miss him especially since we met Alina. Since we met Alina, I don't think about Alina anymore, because since then she has been nothing more than an empty boat; since then Alina doesn't matter; since then the only important thing is what was before, and to miss what was before, that's ... that's not easy to endure."

"I know," Blank said and stroked my hair. We were silent for a while; all you could hear was the rain that had rushed everything forward.

"Presumably there is no end to it," Blank said then. "Presumably there is no end to it as long as you live."

I looked up, at Blank's wrinkled neck, the smooth chin that he never had to shave. "But it grows quieter," he said. "I promise you that it grows quieter. Sometimes it's about as quiet as a song that a neighbor is listening to in the apartment next door."

I detached myself from Blank's hug and blew my nose in Armin's knee sock. "Does he listen to it often?"

Blank smiled. "Yes. Very often. Unfortunately, it's his favorite song. The most beautiful song, he thinks, that was ever written."

"The idiot," I said. "Does he listen to it with the volume on low?"

Blank nodded. "With the volume on low. Most of the time."

I stood up and walked to the window, far away from the bed, far away from Blank, and looked at him from there. The wind blew the rain through the open window into the room. Drops fell on my back and clapped on the floorboards.

"It's like this," I said. 'You can't go away. We have to prevent that."

It was now almost completely dark. Blank's eyes glittered.

"Come back here," he said, patting the bed next to him. "You look exhausted. You're a bit green in the face."

I went to him and sat on the edge of the bed. Blank grabbed me by the shoulders, pressed my upper body onto the bed, lifted up my legs and laid them down, laid me down as if I was a bedridden old woman or a bleary-eyed child. Then he lay down beside me on the side, facing me, and put his head in his hand. He was a bit of green in the face himself, and he looked exhausted, too.

"It's okay if you close your eyes," I said.

"But I don't want to sleep," Blank said.

"It's okay if you sleep. I'll stay awake."

Blank turned over on his back. "But only a little."

"I'll stay awake," I said. "I'll keep watch."

Blank took my hand, closed his eyes and fell asleep in no time.

I looked at his face and rubbed my index finger gently over the bandage on his cheek. I looked down at Blank; there were no new holes. Perhaps, I thought, there was still a little time left.

Blank was fast asleep. I lowered my head; I lay close to Blank, my stomach touched his hip, and because it was hard not to fall asleep, I fell asleep.

When I awoke it was morning. My arm was on Blank's chest. I sat up. Blank was still asleep; He had wrapped himself in a blanket. I stroked his hair. "Blank, do we want to get up?" I whispered.

"Okay" Blank muttered, and turned on his side.

I climbed out of bed, went into the spotless kitchen and made two banana shakes. When I came back with a breakfast tray on my arm, the bed was empty.

"Blank?" I yelled. I yelled a little louder than I wanted.

"I'm here in the bathroom," Blank said. He had put a leg on the edge of the bathtub and was polishing his shoes; they had grown dirty during the cleaning up. He had his back to me. In his back there were suddenly four new holes, four large holes, all at once; you could see through them. I dug my hands into the tray.

"Good morning," Blank said without turning around, and polished his shoes with a piece of toilet paper. "I've been thinking that today, we could clear out your basement. We can try it anyway. I have bad vision today, oddly enough." The shoes were finally polished. Blank took his foot from the edge of the bathtub, turned and smiled at me.

"How are you?" he asked. "Did you sleep well?"

I dropped the tray and pressed my hand against my mouth. Blank took a step back. "What?" he asked. He said it much louder than he may have wanted.

"Your eye," I whispered. Blank walked toward me over the broken fragments and took my hand from my mouth. "What?"

"Your eye," I said.

Blank's right eye was not there anymore. Where his right eye had been was a hole; you could see through it. Blank was pale. He took off his glasses, touched his face and then held his palm in front of the hole. His mouth twisted; his left eye was wide open. Blank made no sound.

I put my hand on Blank's hand and tried to loosen it, but Blank pressed more firmly on his face.

I ran both my hands through his hair. "I know what we'll do," I said quickly. "We'll buy an eye patch. I am sure that there are eye patches at the pharmacy. That's a good idea, Blank, isn't it?"

Blank was silent and looked at me as if it was not him who had lost an eye, but me. Tears ran down his left cheek.

"We'll do that, right Blank? We want to get going right away, don't you think? And afterwards we'll muck out the basement or whatever you want to muck out; we could also still clean a bit." I looked around. "There, for example." I pointed to the dirty bathroom window. "Or here." I yanked open the mirrored cabinet; Q-tips and bandages and my toothbrush fell out and into the sink. "We haven't even cleaned the inside of this at all, Blank. What do you think? And we also need to go shopping." I looked at Blank; he was crying silently. "We have, in fact," I said, stroking him on the arm as if I wanted to brush something away, "in fact we still don't have everything for the child; I did my research in one of these books. we forgot baby nail scissors and a baby bathtub; You'll laugh, Blank—those are essential things, because the nails of babies, I've read, grow very quickly, and they enjoy bathing very much; you'll laugh—people need a tub badly from the beginning, because they like to bathe in it from the beginning, Blank; regarding the eye patch, I think, perhaps we should go to my eye doctor and not to the pharmacy. What do you think?"

Blank stood there; he looked at me and did not move. "Or to a costume shop. There's got to be one somewhere; surely they have eye patches; or you know what, we'll just stick a Band-Aid on it; we had a positive experience with the Band-Aids, and tonight I had a really good idea, by the way. We'll go to see your wife again, Blank. And this time you'll wait downstairs and I'll go up, in the normal way; I'll take the stairs. Of course you can come along too, but if you…after your … last unfortunate visit, if you prefer to wait downstairs, I'll go alone. I'll take the stairs; I'll ring at your wife's door and introduce myself and sit down with your wife at the kitchen table, and then I'll tell her about you. Blank, why didn't we think of it earlier! Perfect, right? I'll tell her about you; you just write down for me everything that you wanted to tell her. Make a list, Blank, and I'll simply tell her everything that you wanted to tell her. Perfect, right? And I'll tell her that you saved my life, and I can also take this opportunity to find out if she has left the oven on again." Blank took the hand away from his face and locked me in his arms; he held me so tightly that my mouth was pressed against his chest and I could say almost nothing else.

"Perfect, right?" I said into Blank's shirt, and then I burst into tears. Blank didn't release me. I sobbed; my whole body was shaking; I slipped a hand between Blank and myself and put it on my belly, because when you are shaking during pregnancy, the one inside probably has to shake with you.

Blank's chin rested on my head. "Close your eyes," he said quietly.

I released myself from Blank's embrace. That wasn't easy; he held me very tightly.

I looked at Blank, his narrow face; the bandage on his left cheek that had come loose at the edges because it had gotten wet, because tears were running across it, his left eye—the eye that was still there, that was still there now.

"No," I said.

Blank smiled at me. "Close your eyes."

I thought about Jacob in the hospital, about Jacob, shortly before he died, about how he wanted to open his eye, how he kept trying to keep his eye open; about Jacob's eyelid, which, despite all his attempts lowered itself over his eye again and again, like the wings of a very tired bird; I thought about how Jacob had not been able to keep his eye open, how it had finally closed altogether, shortly after Jacob had said, "Something funny has happened to me."

Blank stood behind me, grabbed me by the shoulders and leaned my back against his chest. We were now close to each other in the bathroom mirror. Blank cleared his throat. Then he laid a hand over my eyes, the way you put your hand over the eyes of a child on his birthday. His hand was warm. I could no longer see.

"Now," Blank whispered. I felt sick, I gulped. My legs felt like they were filled with air. The pressure of his hand over my eyes was heavier at first, and then it slowly eased, and also Blank's body that had been standing behind me slowly eased.

"Now," said Blank, and then he disappeared. I did not open my eyes for a long time. When I opened them, there was just me in the mirror. Below, on the sink, was an envelope.

I sat on the edge of the tub. All of a sudden I was exceptionally heavy, heavier than I had ever been. As heavy as a bouncer, a woman at the end of a pregnancy with triplets, a fully loaded boat, as heavy as a larger than life flamingo made of reinforced concrete, three African crocodiles, a bus full of Indian yogis, a home, a landscape. As heavy as an old, very friendly man with heavy bones.

I turned the envelope over in my hands. It said "Katja Wiesberg" on the front. The back said "Blank." Before I opened the envelope, I looked out the window. It was, for a morning in April, remarkably bright.

Karate

I'm sitting here with my wife. She cannot see me. That is ~~horrifying~~ not, to be precise, surprising. I will now write you a list; I don't know what else to do.

1.
It would be good if you could love someone you can reveal your true self to. And not only once you are dead.

2.
If possible, don't wander around like a ghost anymore. You have wandered around like a ghost long enough. Wandering around like a ghost leads only in exceptional cases to something good (for example, me to you).

3.
Please tell Armin that I don't know how it is in general to die; I have no idea what it's like to be murdered, to die in a fire, in a car accident, or by drowning. I think when you die the fear of dying also dies. At the moment of my death, death was over. And the fear was gone. It was, in my case, like being in an airplane flying through turbulence. An amazing feeling, as if you were being lifted up from within, although you are standing still. That's the last thing I remember: a feeling of astonishment.

I surmise that the horrors of death are an insinuation of life. The bad thing isn't that death pulls on one end, but that life won't let go at the other (we're grateful for that, too).

4.

Being dead is a matter of course (unless you wander around like a ghost). Death, it seems to me anyway, is very obvious. Life is absurd, including that callous remover.

5.

All hearts are movable. Clamping it really tight is necessary only in exceptional cases; a doctor will decide.

6.

Uncle Arno is the opposite of Uncle Arno and simultaneously Uncle Arno! The same applies to Armin and McQuincey; it applies to you, to Jacob, and to me.

7.

I hope that I can stay with you until the birth of your child. I do not know much about births. If it is about the same as with my wife, my widow, rather, it could proceed as follows: You may think that you will die from it, but with a probability bordering on certainty that will not be the case. You will not die from it. It will be awfully painful, and no one can say how long it will last. If you're unlucky, the staff will not be particularly helpful, because one rarely has the good fortune to encounter someone like Jacob, who knew, as a doctor at least, how to soothe something. But the good thing is that during the birth you are allowed to use your fists, and I would recommend it. At the time, my wife (she is sitting just across from me) administered seemingly unintentional uppercuts. One, when the doctor said: "Don't scream like that;" one when the midwife said, "Others have managed this quite well in the past," and one when the stand-in midwife said: "There has never been a child left inside before." (You don't have to remember these sentences. There may be other equally good occasions.) It's okay if you do it. Just strike.

8.

And then it's done. The child may possibly look bluish, but it will have all the signs of life, including a heart, that will sound like a broken dishwasher. And you will face this in all likelihood with a love that will knock you out. (If not, it's not too bad.)

9.

Nothing lasts forever, except for the utterly extraordinary Nofking. He lives, I suspect, in a country that begins with X.

10.

Karate movies are better than their reputation.

11.

All important decisions must be made on the basis of incomplete data. (I don't know how many opportunities I will have to repeat it; I think one must tell you that more often; you are a bit ~~obtuse~~ stubborn.)

12.

If, like so often, you have the impression that it is inhospitable inside you, this is a symptom that you have worried too much about the interior of others.

13.

Since I'm talking about interiors: you are mistaken. Jacob did not take everything. That which belongs to you, he left behind.

14.

Try, the next time you have a fear of heights, not to hang on for dear life, but to continue standing without support. That would be an exercise in surrender. Surrender is—I can assure you from my position—sooner or later inevitable. Therefore, you can just as well practice it when you have the chance.

15.

Don't let yourself be talked into believing otherwise. Your translations are incredibly creative.

16.

If I know you, you are afraid you will never again enter into a love relationship without reservation, should a new one ever present itself. You are probably right about that. To be precise, only a very few can.

17.

I've always believed that life is an invitation with place cards. As if you, if only for reasons of courtesy, would have to sit in the chair which you have been assigned, even if it's much livelier at the other end of the table. I want to tell you: That is a mistake. It is an invitation with open seating.

18.

~~I am very grateful to you I cannot say enough to you You are~~ I love you, too.

19.

Soon it will be over. Remember Jacob's sign.

20.

~~I wish I could say.~~ See you later. I'll pick you up.